T0022215

"A colossal achievement . . . a genre-c⟨ dream of novels that appeal to ha⟨⟨⟨⟨ ⟨⟨⟨⟨⟨⟨ seeking one big book to last a holiday, and that is what Zafón's quartet has delivered. His trick is to have linked multiple genres— fantasy, historical, romance, metafictional, police-procedural, and political—through prose of atmospheric specificity."

—*The Guardian*

"Carlos Ruiz Zafón is a gifted storyteller who knows how to capture his readers' attention. Packed with suspense, *The Labyrinth of the Spirits* is a gripping edge-of-your-seat thriller. As you read this chilling thriller, you feel as if your pounding heart is missing a beat." —*Washington Book Review*

"Intricate and sublime."

—*O, The Oprah Magazine*, 15 Favorite Books of 2018

"A mystery, a love letter to books, and a magical adventure all wrapped up in one, this book is a masterful work of literature that will invigorate your love of reading." —*Bustle*

"A gripping and moving thriller set in Franco's Spain that's fully accessible to newcomers. . . . Twenty-nine-year-old Alicia Gris, a capable, insightful operative working for the Spanish secret police . . . will remind readers of Lisbeth Salander. . . . Fans of complex and literate mysteries featuring detectives with integrity working under oppressive and corrupt regimes will be well satisfied." —*Publishers Weekly*, starred review

"Ruiz Zafón clearly has had a great deal of fun in pulling this vast story together. . . . His ability to keep track of a thousand threads while, in the end, celebrating the power of storytelling is admirable. . . . A satisfying conclusion to a grand epic that, of course, will only leave its fans wanting more."

—*Kirkus Reviews*, starred review

"A compelling, multifaceted, and haunting work of art told by a master storyteller. To say that the writing is brilliant is an understatement. Carlos Ruiz Zafón respects every word, taking his time to develop and do justice to the major, minor, and irrelevant characters, places, things, or situations in order to recreate a dark time in Spain's history and ensure that the reader not only bears witness to it but is immersed in it and feels it. . . . An epic novel that is also an ode to writing and to the undying thirst for knowledge through reading."   —*Historical Novel Society*

"Gothic, operatic, and in many ways old-fashioned, this is a story about storytelling and survival, with the horrors of Francoist Spain present on every page. Compelling . . . this is for readers who savor each word and scene, soaking in the ambience of Barcelona, Zafón's greatest character (after, perhaps, the irrepressible Fermín Romero de Torres)."   —*Booklist*

"*The Labyrinth of the Sprits* is the sublime culmination to a truly outstanding series. Set in Barcelona from 1938 through the 1970s, these books deftly combine the world of bookselling, the long shadow of the Spanish Civil War, gothic literary interplay, wonderfully salty characters, sublime dialogue and verbal sparring, along with elaborate and satisfying exposition. Taken together or individually they represent a reading experience not to be missed. . . . Reading *Labyrinth* first would have given a sublime insight into any of the other books. . . . As long as you actually open a door to the labyrinth and enter it, all is well. As to not reading the Cemetery of Forgotten books at all, that is obviously a grave error."
—Barnes & Nobles

"Zafón's vision is one of the complexity of human experience, reveling in language."   —*Sydney Morning Herald* (Australia)

"Zafón is a master storyteller, combining the postmodern and the traditional in an enchanting hymn to literature. . . . Magnificent. . . . A dizzying tale of drama, intrigue, and passion."
—*Mail on Sunday* (UK)

PRAISE FOR
The Shadow of the Wind

"If you thought the true gothic novel died with the nineteenth century, this will change your mind. *The Shadow of the Wind* is the real deal. . . . This is one gorgeous read."   —Stephen King

"Anyone who enjoys novels that are scary, erotic, touching, tragic, and thrilling should rush right out to the nearest bookstore and pick up *The Shadow of the Wind*. Really, you should."
—*Washington Post*

"Wondrous . . . masterful. . . . A love letter to literature, intended for readers as passionate about storytelling as its young hero."
—*Entertainment Weekly,* Editor's Choice

"Gabriel García Márquez meets Umberto Eco meets Jorge Luis Borges for a sprawling magic show. . . . His novel eddies in currents of passion, revenge, and mysteries whose layers peel away onionlike yet persist in growing back. At times these mysteries take on the aspect of the supernatural. The figures appear beleaguered by ghosts until these give way to something even more frightening: the creak of real floors undermined by real rot and the inexorability of human destinies grimmer than any ghostly one could be. . . . We are taken on a wild ride that executes hairpin bends with breathtaking lurches."
—*New York Times Book Review*

"This novel has it all: seduction, danger, revenge, and a mystery, that the author teases with mastery. Zafón has outdone even the mighty Charles Dickens."   —*Philadelphia Inquirer*

THE
CITY
OF
MIST

ALSO BY CARLOS RUIZ ZAFÓN

THE CEMETERY OF FORGOTTEN BOOKS

The Shadow of the Wind
The Angel's Game
The Prisoner of Heaven
The Labyrinth of the Spirits

The Prince of Mist
The Midnight Palace
The Watcher in the Shadows
Marina

THE
CITY
OF
MIST

Stories

CARLOS RUIZ ZAFÓN

Translated by from Spanish by Lucia Graves
With two stories translated by Carlos Ruiz Zafón
And one story written in English by Carlos Ruiz Zafón

HARPER ⬤ PERENNIAL

NEW YORK • LONDON • TORONTO • SYDNEY • NEW DELHI • AUCKLAND

HARPER ● PERENNIAL

FIRST US EDITION

Library of Congress Cataloging-in-Publication Data has been applied for.

ISBN 978-0-06-311809-6

21 22 23 24 25   LSC   10 9 8 7 6 5 4 3 2 1

Soon afterwards, like figures made of mist, father and son disappear into the crowd of the Ramblas, their steps lost forever in the shadow of the wind.

The Shadow of the Wind

CONTENTS

BLANCA AND THE DEPARTURE

(FROM THE IMAGINED MEMOIRS
OF ONE DAVID MARTÍN)

Translated by Lucia Graves

I

I've always envied the ease with which some people are able to forget – people for whom the past is only a set of last season's clothes or a pair of old shoes that can simply be condemned to the back of a cupboard to ensure they're unable to retrace lost footsteps. I had the misfortune of remembering everything, and that everything in turn, remembered me. I recall my early childhood days of cold and loneliness, of dead moments spent gazing at greyness; and the dark mirror that haunted my father's eyes. Yet I can barely bring back the memory of a single friend. I can conjure up the faces of children in the Ribera neighbourhood with whom I sometimes played or quarrelled in the street, but none I would wish to rescue from that land of indifference. None except Blanca's.

Blanca was about two years older than me. I met her one day in April outside my front door. She was walking hand in hand with a maid who had come to collect some books from a small antiquarian bookshop, opposite the building site for the concert hall. By a quirk of fate the bookshop didn't open until twelve o'clock that day and the maid had arrived at eleven thirty, leaving a half-hour gap during which, unbeknown to me, my fate was about to be sealed. Had it been up to me, I would never have dared exchange a single word with her. Her clothes, her smell and her elegant bearing spoke of a wealthy girl cosseted by silks and velvet; she clearly didn't belong to my world, and even less did I belong to hers. We were separated by only a few metres of street and miles of invisible laws. I merely gazed at her, the way one admires objects that have been consigned to a glass cabinet or to the display window of one of those shops that may look open, but you know you'll never enter. I've often thought that, were it not for my father's firm strictures regarding my personal cleanliness, Blanca would never have noticed me. My father was of the opinion that he'd seen enough filth during the war to fill nine lives and although we were as poor as church mice, he had taught me, from a very early age, to become used to the freezing water that ran – when it felt like it – from the tap above the sink, and to those soap bars that smelled of bleach and scraped everything off you, even your regrets. That is how, when I'd just turned eight, yours truly, David Martín, a clean nonentity and a future candidate for third-rate author, managed to gather enough composure not to look away when that well-to-do doll set her eyes on me and smiled timidly. My father had always told me that in life one should pay people back in kind. He was referring to slaps in the face and other such offences, but I decided to follow his teachings and return that smile – and while I was at it, throw in a small nod. She was the one who walked over, slowly and, looking me up and down, held out her hand, a gesture nobody had ever made to me, and said:

'My name is Blanca.'

Blanca held out her hand the way young ladies do in drawing-room comedy, palm down and with the detachment of a Parisian damsel. I didn't realise that what was expected of me was to lean forward and brush her hand with my lips, and after a while Blanca removed her hand and raised an eyebrow.

'I'm David.'

'Are you always so bad-mannered?'

I was working on a rhetorical way out that would compensate for my uncouth plebeian background, rescuing my image with a display of ingenuity and wit, when the maid walked over, a look of alarm on her face, and stared at me the way one stares at a rabid dog let loose on the street. She was a young, severe-looking woman with deep, dark eyes that held no sympathy for me. Grabbing Blanca by the arm, she pulled her out of reach.

'Who are you speaking to, Miss Blanca? You know your father doesn't like you to talk to strangers.'

'He's not a stranger, Antonia. This is my friend David. My father knows him.'

I froze while the maid studied me out of the corner of her eye.

'David what?'

'David Martín, madam. At your service.'

'Nobody is at Antonia's service, David. She's the one who serves us. Isn't that right, Antonia?'

It was just an instant, an expression nobody would have noticed but me – for I was watching her closely. Antonia darted a brief, dark glance at Blanca, a look that was poisoned with hatred and turned my blood to ice, before she concealed it with a smile of resignation and a shake of the head, playing down the matter.

'Kids,' she muttered under her breath as she turned to walk back to the bookshop, which was now opening its doors.

Blanca then made as if to sit down on the front doorstep. Even a yokel like me knew that the dress she wore could not come into contact with the base materials covered in soot with which my home was built. I took off my patched-up jacket and spread it over the step like a doormat. Blanca sat on my best garment, gazing at the street and the people walking by. From the bookshop door, Antonia didn't take her eyes off us, and I pretended not to notice.

'Do you live here?' Blanca asked.

I nodded, pointing at the adjacent building.

'Do you?'

Blanca looked at me as if that were the stupidest question she'd heard in her short life.

'Of course not.'

'Don't you like the neighbourhood?'

'It smells bad, it's dark and cold and the people are ugly and noisy.'

It had never occurred to me to size up the world I knew in such a way, but I found no solid arguments with which to contradict her.

'So why do you come here?'

'My father has a house near the Born Market. Antonia brings me here to visit him almost every day.'

'And where do you live?'

'In Sarriá, with my mother.'

Even a poor wretch like me had heard of Sarriá, but I'd never actually been there. I imagined it as a sort of citadel made up of large mansions and lime-tree avenues, luxurious carriages and leafy gardens, a world inhabited by people like that girl, only taller. Hers was a perfumed, luminous world, no doubt, a world of fresh breezes and good-looking, quiet citizens.

'So how come your father lives here and not with you and your mother?'

Blanca shrugged and looked away. The subject seemed to make her uncomfortable so I decided not to insist.

'It's just for a while,' she added. 'He'll come back home soon.'

'Of course,' I said, without quite knowing what we were talking about, but adopting that commiserating tone of those already born defeated, experts at recommending resignation.

'The Ribera isn't that bad, you'll see. You'll get used to it.'

'I don't want to get used to it. I don't like this neighbourhood, nor the house my father has bought. I don't have any friends here.'

I gulped.

'I can be your friend, if you like.'

'And who are you?'

'David Martín.'

'You've already said that.'

'I suppose I'm also someone who doesn't have any friends.'

Blanca turned her head to look at me with a mixture of curiosity and hesitation.

'I don't like playing hide-and-seek, or ball games,' she warned me.

'Neither do I.'

Blanca smiled and held out her hand again. This time I did my utmost to brush it with my lips.

'Do you like stories?' she asked.

'That's what I like best in the whole world.'

'I know a few stories that very few people have heard,' she said. 'My father writes them for me.'

'I also write stories. Well, I invent them and learn them by heart.'

Blanca frowned.

'Let's see. Tell me one.'

'Now?'

She nodded, defiantly.

'I hope it's not about little princesses,' she threatened. 'I hate little princesses.'

'Well, it does have one princess . . . but she's a very bad one.'

Blanca's face lit up.

'How bad?'

2

That morning Blanca became my first reader, my first audience. I told her, as best I could, my story about princesses and sorcerers, maledictions and poisoned kisses in a universe of spells and living palaces that slithered along a misty wilderness like infernal beasts. When the narrative came to an end and the heroine had sunk into the frozen waters of a black lake holding a cursed rose in her hands, Blanca set the course of my life forever: moved with emotion, she shed a tear and, casting aside any high-flown airs, murmured that she thought my story was beautiful. I would have given my life for that moment never to disappear. Antonia's shadow stretching over our feet brought me back to the humdrum reality.

'We're going now, Miss Blanca. Your father doesn't like us to be late for lunch.'

The maid snatched her away and led her down the street, but I held Blanca's gaze until her figure vanished and I saw her waving at me. I picked up my jacket and put it on again, feeling Blanca's warmth and aroma over me. Then I smiled to myself and, although it was just for a few seconds, I became aware that for the first time in my life I was happy, and that after tasting that poison my existence would never be the same again.

That night, while we were having our dinner of soup and bread, my father looked at me severely.

'You seem different,' he said. 'Has something happened?'

'No, Father.'

I went to bed early, fleeing from his irritable mood. I lay down on my bed in the dark, thinking about Blanca, about the stories I wanted to invent for her, and I realised that I didn't know where she lived or when, if ever, I was going to see her again.

I spent several days searching for Blanca. After lunch, as soon as my father fell asleep or closed his bedroom door, succumbing to his personal oblivion, I would go out and head for the lower part of the neighbourhood, where I'd walk through the dark, narrow side streets surrounding Paseo del Borne in the hope of finding Blanca or her sinister maid. I managed to memorise every hidden corner and every shadow of that labyrinth of streets whose walls seemed to lean against one another and blend into a network of tunnels. The ancient lanes of the medieval guilds formed a web of corridors that commenced at the basilica of Santa María del Mar and then intertwined to form a knot of incomprehensible passages, arches and curves where the sun barely penetrated more than a few minutes a day. Gargoyles and relief sculptures marked the crossings where old, ruined palaces met buildings that grew, one on top of the other, like rocks forming a cliff edge of windows and towers. In the evening I would return home exhausted just as my father was waking up.

On the sixth day, when I was beginning to think that I'd dreamed that encounter, I walked up Calle de los Mirallers towards the side entry of Santa María del Mar. A thick mist had dropped over the city and was creeping through the streets like a silvery veil. The church door was open and there I saw two figures, both dressed in white – a woman and a girl – silhouetted against the arched entrance. A second later the mist had wrapped them in an embrace. I ran to the door and stepped inside the basilica. The draught dragged the mist into the building and a ghostly mantle of vapour, glowing in the candlelight, floated over the pews in the nave. I spied Antonia, the maid, kneeling by one of the confessionals, her expression contrite and pleading. I was sure that harpy's confession had the colouring and consistency of tar. Blanca was sitting in one of the pews, waiting, her legs dangling, staring absently at the altar. I walked over to the end of the pew and she turned her head. When she saw me her face lit up and she smiled, making me instantly forget the endless days of misery I'd spent trying to find her. I sat down next to her.

'What are you doing here?' she asked.

'I was coming to mass,' I improvised.

'It's not the time for mass,' she laughed.

I didn't want to lie to her, so I just lowered my eyes. There was no need to say anything.

'I've also missed you,' she said. 'I thought you might have forgotten me.'

I shook my head. The hazy atmosphere and the muffled whispers emboldened me and I blurted out a declaration I'd devised for one of my tales about magic and heroism.

'I would never be able to forget you,' I said.

Those were words that would have sounded empty and ridiculous, except when spoken by an eight-year-old boy who probably didn't know what he was saying, but felt it. Blanca looked into my eyes with a strange sadness that did not belong to a child's gaze, and she pressed my hand firmly.

'Promise you'll never forget me.'

Antonia, the maid, now apparently free of sin and ready to re-offend, was observing us with hostility from the end of the pew.

'Miss Blanca?'

Blanca kept her eyes fixed on mine.

'Promise.'

'I promise.'

Once again the maid took away my only friend. I saw them walk down the nave and disappear through the back door that led to Paseo del Borne. But this time a touch of malice suffused my melancholy. Something told me that the maid was a woman with a fragile conscience who regularly visited the confessional to purge her faults. The church bells struck four o'clock and the germ of a plan began to form in my mind.

From that day on, every afternoon at a quarter to four I would go to Santa María del Mar and sit in one of the pews near the confessionals. I only had to wait two days before they reappeared. I waited for the maid to kneel down in front of the confessional and then stepped over to where Blanca was standing.

'Every other day at four,' she whispered.

Without wasting a second I grabbed her hand and took her on a tour of the basilica. I'd prepared a story for her that took place precisely there, among the columns and chapels of the church, with a final duel between an evil spirit made of ashes and blood, and a heroic knight, fought in the crypt beneath the altar. It would become the first episode of a series of finely detailed adventures, terrors and romances that I invented for Blanca, titled *The Cathedral Ghosts* and which, with my immense vanity as a novice author, seemed to me near perfection. I finished recounting the first episode just in time for us to get back to the confessional and meet up with the maid, who didn't see me this time because I hid behind a pillar. For a couple of weeks Blanca and I met there every other day. We shared our kids' stories and dreams, while the maid tortured the parish priest with exhaustive accounts of her sins.

At the end of the second week the confessor, a priest who looked liked a retired boxer, noticed my presence and quickly put two and two together. I was about to slip away when he beckoned me to approach the confessional. His pugilistic appearance convinced me and I hastened to obey. I knelt down, trembling in the knowledge that my ruse had been discovered.

'Hail Mary, full of grace,' I murmured through the latticed opening.

'Do I look like a nun to you, you little rascal?'

'I'm sorry, Father. I wasn't sure what I was meant to say.'

'Don't they teach you this at school?'

'The teacher is an atheist and says you priests are an instrument of the capitalist system.'

'And what's he an instrument of?'

'He didn't say. I think he considers himself a free agent.'

The priest laughed.

'Where did you learn to speak like that? In school?'

'Reading.'

'Reading what?'

'Whatever I can.'

'And do you read the word of the Lord?'

'Does the Lord write?'

'Keep acting like a smart aleck and you'll end up burning in hell.'

I gulped.

'Do I have to tell you my sins now?' I whispered anxiously.

'There's no need. They're stamped on your forehead. What's this business that's going on with the maid and the girl almost every day?'

'What business?'

'Let me remind you that this is a confessional and if you lie to a priest Our Lord may well strike you down with a deadly bolt on your way out,' the confessor threatened.

'Are you sure?'

'If I were you I wouldn't risk it. Come on, spit it out.'

'Where do I begin?'

'Skip the playing with yourself and the swear words and tell me what it is you do every day in my parish at four o'clock in the afternoon.'

The kneeling, the darkness and the smell of wax have something about them that invite one to unburden one's conscience. I even confessed my first sneeze. The priest listened in silence, clearing his throat every time I stopped. At the end of my confession, when I supposed he was going to send me straight to hell, I heard him chuckling.

'Aren't you going to give me a penance?'

'What's your name, kid?'

'David Martín, sir.'

'It's "father", not "sir". One would say "sir" to your father, and "Lord" to the Most High. But I'm not your father, I'm *a* father, in this case, Father Sebastián.'

'Forgive me, Father Sebastián.'

'Just "father" will be fine. And the one who forgives is the Lord. I only do the administering. Now: back to business. For today I'll let you go with only a warning and a couple of Hail Marys. And as I believe that the Lord, in his infinite wisdom, has chosen this most unusual path to persuade you to come to church, I'll offer you a deal. Every other day, half an hour before you meet up with your little damsel, you come and help me clean the sacristy. In exchange I'll keep the maid here for at least half an hour to give you more time.'

'You'll do this for me, Father?'

'*Ego te absolvo in nomine Patris et Filii et Spiritus Sancti.* And now clear off.'

3

Father Sebastián proved to be a man of his word. I would arrive half an hour early and help him in the sacristy, for the poor fellow was almost lame and could barely manage on his own. He liked to listen to my stories, which according to him were little blasphemies of a venial nature, but which amused him, especially the ones about ghosts and curses. He seemed to me as solitary a person as I was, and when I admitted that Blanca was my only friend, he agreed to help me. I lived for those meetings.

Blanca always arrived looking pallid and cheerful, dressed in ivory-coloured clothes. She always wore new shoes and necklaces with silver medals. She listened to the tales I invented for her and told me about her world and the large dark house, close by, where her father had gone to live, a frightening place she loathed. Sometimes she talked about her mother, Alicia, with whom she lived in the old family house in Sarriá. Other times, speaking almost in tears, she mentioned her father, whom she adored but who, she said, was ill and now barely left the house.

'My father is a writer,' she explained. 'Like you. But he doesn't write stories for me any more, the way he used to. Now he only writes stuff for a man who sometimes comes to the house at night to visit him. I've never seen him, but once I spent the night there and I heard them talking until very late, locked up in my father's study. That man isn't good. He scares me.'

Every afternoon, when we parted, I walked back home day-dreaming about the moment when I would rescue her from that existence marked by absences, from that night visitor who scared her, from that pampered life that stole the light from her with every passing day. Every afternoon I told myself that I wasn't going to forget her and that, so long as I remembered her, I'd be able to save her.

One November day – it had dawned blue with frosty windows – I went out to meet her as usual, but Blanca didn't come to our rendezvous. For two weeks I waited in vain for my friend to appear in the basilica. I looked everywhere for her, and when my father caught me weeping at night I lied to him and told him I had toothache, although no tooth could hurt as much as that absence. Father Sebastián, who began to worry every time he saw me waiting there like a lost soul, sat down next to me one day and tried to comfort me.

'Perhaps you should forget your friend, David.'

'I can't. I promised I would never forget her.'

A month had gone by since her disappearance when I noticed I was beginning to forget her. I'd stopped going to the church every other day, I'd stopped inventing stories for her and holding her image in the dark every night as I fell asleep. I had begun to forget the sound of her voice, her smell and the light of her face. When I realised that I was losing her, I wanted to go and see Father Sebastián to beg his forgiveness, to beg him to pull away the pain that was devouring me, the pain that was telling me to my face that I'd broken my promise and had been incapable of remembering the only friend I'd ever had.

The last time I saw Blanca was at the beginning of that December. I'd gone down to the street and was standing by the front door staring at the rain when I caught sight of her. She was walking alone in the rain, her white patent shoes and her ivory-coloured dress stained with muddy water. I ran towards her and saw that she was weeping. I asked her what had happened and she hugged me. Blanca told me that her father was very ill and that she'd run away from home. I told her not to be afraid, we would run away together. If necessary I'd steal the money to buy two train tickets and we'd leave the city forever. Blanca smiled and embraced me. We stood like that, hugging silently beneath the scaffolding of the concert hall, until a large black carriage appeared through the mist of the downpour and stopped in front of us. A dark figure stepped out of the carriage. It was Antonia, the maid. She pulled Blanca from my arms and shoved her inside the carriage. Blanca screamed and when I tried to grab her arm the maid turned and slapped me as hard as she could. I fell backwards on the cobblestones, dazed by the blow. When I got up again the carriage was moving into the distance.

I ran after the carriage in the rain until I reached the roadworks for the construction of Vía Layetana. The new avenue was a long valley of waterlogged ditches that was destroying the jungle of side streets and houses in the Ribera quarter as it advanced with hammer blows of dynamite and demolition cranes. I saw the carriage dodging potholes and puddles, getting further and further away from me. In an attempt not to lose sight of it I climbed onto a ridge of cobblestones and earth that ran alongside a ditch flooded by the rain. Suddenly I felt the earth give way beneath my feet and I slipped. I tumbled into the ditch, falling face down into the well of water that had collected below. When I managed to stand up and get my head out of the liquid that covered me up to my waist, I realised that the water was poisoned and alive with black spiders that floated and walked over the surface. The insects hurled themselves over me and covered my hands and my arms. I screamed, waving my arms about and climbing up the mud walls of the trench, panic-stricken. By the time I got out of the flooded ditch it was too late. The carriage was disappearing into the upper reaches of the city, its outline enveloped in the blanket of rain. Soaked to my bones I dragged myself back home where my father was still asleep and locked up in his room. I took my clothes off and got into bed trembling with anger and cold. I noticed that my arms were covered in tiny red, bleeding dots. Bites. The spiders in the ditch hadn't wasted their time. I could feel the poison burning in my blood and then I lost consciousness, falling into a crater of darkness somewhere between awareness and sleep.

I dreamed that I was walking through the deserted streets of the neighbourhood looking for Blanca in the storm. Black rain pounded the facades and through flashes of lightning I could make out distant figures. A large black carriage crept along in the fog. Blanca travelled inside the carriage, shouting and banging the windows with her fists. I followed her shouts as far as a narrow, murky street where I saw the carriage come to a halt opposite a tall, dark house – a house that seemed to twist upwards, forming a tower that pierced the sky. Blanca was stepping out of the carriage and looking at me, stretching her pleading hands towards me. I wanted to run to her but my steps would only advance a few metres. It was then that the large, dark silhouette appeared, standing at the door of the house – a huge angel with a face of marble that looked at me and smiled like a wolf, spreading its black wings over Blanca and wrapping her in an embrace. I screamed, but utter silence had descended over the city. During an endless moment the rain was left suspended in mid-air, a million glass tears floating in the void, and I saw the angel kiss her on the forehead, its lips leaving a mark on her skin like that of a red-hot iron. When the rain brushed the ground they had both disappeared forever.

NAMELESS

Translated by Lucia Graves

Years later, I was told that she was last seen walking up that sombre avenue leading to the gates of the Pueblo Nuevo Cemetery. Evening was falling and an icy wind was dragging a cupola of red clouds over the city. She walked alone, shivering with cold and leaving a wake of uncertain footsteps on the mantle of snow that had started to fall in mid-afternoon. When she reached the entrance to the graveyard she paused for a moment to catch her breath. A forest of angels and crosses peered over the walls. The stench of dead flowers, lime and sulphur licked her face, inviting her in. She was about to start walking again when a stabbing pain throbbed through her entrails like a red-hot iron. She put her hands on her belly and took a deep breath, trying to stop the nausea. For an endless moment all she could feel was agony and the fear of being unable to take another step, of collapsing by the entrance to the cemetery and being discovered there at dawn, clinging to its spiked gates like a figure of bile and frost, with the child she was carrying trapped hopelessly in an icy sarcophagus.

It would have been so easy to give in, there and then, stretched out on the snow, and close her eyes forever. But she could feel the breath of life beating inside her, a breath that did not want to be extinguished, that kept her upright, and she knew she would not succumb to the suffering or the cold. She gathered all the strength she didn't possess and got back on her feet. Ribbons of pain knotted themselves in her belly but she ignored them and hastened on. She didn't stop until she'd left the labyrinth of tombs and mouldy statues behind her. Only then, when she raised her head to look, did a ray of hope flash through her: for silhouetted against the murky twilight stood the large wrought-iron door that led to the Old Book Factory.

Further on, the Pueblo Nuevo neighbourhood spread towards a horizon of ashes and shadows. The city of factories outlined the dark reflection of a Barcelona bewitched by hundreds of chimneys that exhaled their black breath over the scarlet of the sky. As the young woman entered the maze of narrow streets entangled among cavernous stores and warehouses, her eyes recognised some of the large structures that shored up the neighbourhood, from the factory of Can Saladrigas to the great water tower. The Old Book Factory stood out among them all. Turrets and hanging bridges emerged from its extravagant profile, suggesting the work of a diabolical architect who had discovered how to flout the laws of perspective. Domes, minarets and chimney stacks seemed to charge through a chaos of vaults and naves supported by dozens of flying buttresses and columns. Sculptures and reliefs snaked along its walls, and rotundas, speckled with windows, sent out shafts of ghostly light.

The girl observed the row of gargoyles along its cornices – they oozed streaks of vapour, spreading a bitter perfume of ink and paper. Feeling another wave of pain coming she hurried to the large front door and pulled the bell rope. The muffled echo of a chime could be heard behind the large wrought-iron door. The girl looked behind her and noticed that in just a few seconds the snow had covered the trail of her footsteps. A cold, biting wind cornered her against the iron door. She pulled the bell rope again, harder and repeatedly, but no answer came. All around her, the faint light seemed to be vanishing with every passing second and shadows began to spread quickly at her feet. Well aware that she was running out of time, she stepped back a little and scanned the large windows of the main facade. A motionless figure was silhouetted against one of the windows with smoked-glass panes, like a spider in the centre of its web. The girl couldn't see its face; all she could make out was a female body, but she knew she was being observed. She waved her arms and called out for help. The figure remained immobile until suddenly the light went out. The window was now in complete darkness, but the girl noticed that the two eyes that had been piercing hers were still there, in the shadow, unmoving, shining in the twilight. For the first time fear made her forget the cold and the pain. She pulled the bell rope a third time and when she realised that ringing the bell would get no response she started shouting and banging the door with her fists. She struck the door until her hands bled and she begged for help until her voice broke and her legs could no longer hold her up. Then she collapsed into an icy puddle, closed her eyes and listened to the throbbing of life in her womb. Soon the snow began to cover her face and her body.

Evening was already spreading like a pool of ink when the door opened, casting a fan of light over the girl. Two figures carrying gas lamps knelt down beside her. One of the men, heavily built and pock-marked, pushed the hair away from her forehead. She opened her eyes and smiled at him. The two men exchanged glances and the second man, who was younger and small, pointed at something shining on the girl's hand. A ring. He was about to snatch it from her but his companion stopped him.

They helped her up. The older and stronger of the two took her in his arms and told the other one to run and get help. The younger man agreed reluctantly and disappeared into the dusk. The girl kept her eyes fixed on those of the heavily built man who was carrying her in his arms, murmuring words that wouldn't form on her cracked lips. *Thank you, thank you.*

The man, who had a slight limp, took her to what looked like a coach house next to the factory entrance. Once they were inside, the girl heard other voices and felt various arms holding her and laying her on a wooden table opposite a fire. Slowly, the heat from the flames melted the frozen beads of ice on her hair and face. Two women, both as young as her and wearing maids' uniforms, wrapped her in a blanket and began to rub her arms and legs. Two hands that smelled of spices brought a glass of hot wine to her lips. The liquid spread through her like a balm.

As she lay on the table, the girl glanced round the room and realised she was in a kitchen. One of the maids placed a few tea towels under her head and the girl tilted her forehead backwards. From this position she could see the room upside down – the pots, frying pans and utensils hanging against gravity. That is how she saw her come in. The pale, serene face of the lady in white was slowly approaching from the door as if she were walking on the ceiling. The maids stood aside as she went by and the heavily built man looked down fearfully and quickly moved out of the way. The girl heard footsteps and voices leaving the room and sensed she was now alone with the lady in white. She saw her bend over her and felt her warm, sweet breath.

'Don't be afraid,' whispered the lady.

The lady was studying her quietly with her grey eyes; the back of her hand, the softest skin the girl had ever known, brushed her cheek. It occurred to the girl that the lady had the presence and the manners of a broken angel, fallen from heaven amid forgotten cobwebs. She searched her eyes for protection. The

lady smiled at her and stroked her face with infinite tenderness. They remained like that for almost half an hour, almost
in silence, until she heard loud voices in the courtyard and the
maids returned, together with the younger man and a gentleman wearing a thick coat and carrying a large black doctor's
bag. The doctor stood by her side and proceeded to take her
pulse. His eyes observed her nervously. He prodded her belly
and sighed. The girl struggled to understand the orders the
doctor was giving the maids and the male servants who had
gathered round the fire. Only then did she find the strength
to recover her voice and ask whether her child would be born
in good health. The doctor who, judging from his expression,
thought neither of them would live, merely exchanged a look
with the lady in white.

'David,' murmured the girl. 'He'll be called David.'

The lady nodded and kissed the girl on her forehead.

'Now you must be strong,' whispered the lady, holding her
hand firmly.

Years later I learned that that girl, who was barely seventeen,
lay completely silent, without uttering even a whimper, her eyes
open and tears falling down her cheeks while the doctor opened
her belly with a scalpel and brought a child into the world, a boy
who would only be able to remember her through the words of
strangers. Time and time again I've wondered whether she ever
saw the lady in white as she turned her back on her to take the
baby and hold it close, cuddling it against her white silk chest
while she, the girl, stretched her arms out and begged to be
allowed to see her child. I've often wondered whether that girl
was able to hear the sound of her son crying as he was taken
away in the arms of another woman and she was left alone in
that room where she lay in a pool of her own blood until they
returned to wrap her body, still trembling, in a shroud. I've

wondered whether she felt how one of the maids struggled with the ring on her left hand, tearing her skin to steal it from her while they dragged her body back into the night, and the two men who had rescued her now loaded it into a cart. I've asked myself so many times whether she was still breathing when the horses stopped and the two individuals took the shroud and flung it into the gully that dragged the sewage from a hundred factories towards the tundra of cardboard-and-reed shacks that covered the Bogatell beach.

I've wanted to believe that at that last moment, when the putrid waters spat her into the sea and the shroud that wrapped her unfolded in the current to deliver her body into the darkness of the deep, she knew that the boy she had given birth to would live and would always remember her.

I never knew her name.

That girl was my mother.

A YOUNG LADY FROM BARCELONA

Translated by Lucia Graves

Laia was five years old the first time her father sold her. It was an innocent, kind-hearted arrangement, with no malice other than that inspired by hunger and pressing debts. Eduardo Sentís, a hapless, penniless portrait photographer, had just inherited the studio of the man who had been his mentor and boss for over twenty years. He had started work there as an unpaid trainee, had then become an assistant and finally, after obtaining the required qualifications, though not the salary, had moved on to become photographer and junior manager. The studio's premises occupied a spacious ground floor on Calle Consejo de Ciento and consisted of four sets, two developing rooms and a storage room bursting with out-of-date equipment in a dilapidated state. Aside from the studio, Eduardo had also inherited the numerous unpaid bills left by his boss, who had been more of a man of lenses and plates than one of clarity in his accounts. At the time of his boss's demise, Eduardo Sentís had not received his wages for over six months. In the words of the executor, the post-mortem takeover of the business and the miserable inheritance that came with it were supposed to be a just reward for his loyal and austere dedication. But as soon as light and accountants fell on the company's business books, Eduardo Sentís realised that what his boss had left him in return for having offered him his youth and his efforts was no inheritance but a simple curse. He had to fire all the employees and confront the survival of the studio, and his own survival, alone. Until then, a large part of the business generated by the studio focused on family celebrations of various kinds, from weddings and christenings to funerals and Holy Communions. Work related to funeral parlours and burials were a speciality of the house, and over time Eduardo Sentís had found it easier to light and photograph the deceased than the living. The dead never looked out of focus in long exposures because they didn't move or have to hold their breath.

It was his reputation as a photographer of bereavement that secured him a job which, at first sight, seemed straightforward and uncomplicated. Margarita Pons, the five-year-old daughter of a wealthy married couple with a mansion on Avenida del Tibidabo and an industrial estate on the banks of the River Ter, had died from some strange fever on New Year's day of 1901. Her mother, Doña Eulalia, had suffered a nervous breakdown which the family doctors had hastened to mitigate with generous doses of laudanum. Don Federico Pons, paterfamilias and a gentleman with no room or time for sentimentalities, who had seen more than one of his children die, did not shed a tear or utter a groan. He already had a healthy and talented first-born heir. The loss of a daughter, for all its sadness, also meant an obvious saving in family expenditure, both long- and medium-term. What Don Federico wanted was to hold the funeral service without delay, followed by the burial in the family vault in Montjuïc Cemetery, so that he could resume his daily work routine as soon as possible. But Doña Eulalia, a fragile creature who was prone to the influence of the sinister ladies of The Light, a spiritualist society on Calle Elisabets, was in no fit state to turn the page as resolutely as her husband. In order to silence her sighs, Don Federico allowed her to have a series of photographs taken of the deceased princess before the undertakers proceeded with the body's eternal consignment to an ivory coffin adorned with pieces of blue glass.

Eduardo Sentís, photographer of the dead, was summoned to the Pons family mansion on Avenida del Tibidabo. The property lay hidden inside a dense grove accessed through a wrought-iron gate on the corner of the avenue and Calle José Garí. It was a grey, grim day, a sliver of that harsh, misty winter that had brought such bad luck on poor Sentís. As he didn't have anyone with whom to leave his daughter Laia, he took her with him. Holding the girl with one hand and his lens-and-bellows case in the other, Sentís took the blue tram and turned up at the mansion, determined to start the year with some hard cash income. He was welcomed by a servant who led him through the garden to the house, where he was shown to a small waiting room. Laia was fascinated by everything she saw, because she'd never seen a place like that. It looked like something straight out of a fairy tale, but one of those about an evil stepmother and mirrors that were poisoned by bad memories. Glass chandeliers hung from the ceiling, statues and paintings lined the walls and thick Persian carpets covered the floors. As he gazed at all that weighty fortune, Sentís was tempted to put up his price. He was received by Don Federico, who barely looked at him and addressed him in the tone he reserved for servants and factory workers. He was given an hour to take a set of photographs of the deceased child. When he saw Laia, Don Federico frowned disapprovingly. It was a widely accepted dogma among the males of his family that the utility of the female gender was confined to the bedroom, the table or the kitchen, and that brat had neither the age nor the pedigree to be considered for any of the three. Sentís excused the child's presence claiming that the urgency of the job had not given him enough time to find someone to take care of her. Don Federico sighed unsympathetically and told the photographer to follow him up the stairs.

The little princess had been placed in a room on the first floor. She lay on a wide bed covered in white lilies, her hands crossed over her chest and clutching a crucifix. A tiara of flowers adorned her forehead and she wore a diaphanous silk dress. Two silent male servants guarded the door. A shaft of ashen light from the window fell on the child's face. Her skin, almost transparent, had taken on the colour and appearance of marble, with blue and black veins running through it. Her eyes had sunk into their sockets and her lips were purple. The room stank of dead flowers.

Sentís told Laia to wait in the corridor and began setting up his tripod and camera in front of the bed. He thought he'd create six plates in all. Two close-ups with one of the long lenses, two mid-range shots from the waist up and a couple of general, full-body shots. All from the same angle, because he suspected that a profile or a three-quarter shot would draw attention to the web of veins and dark capillaries under the girl's skin and produce pictures that might look more sinister than the situation required. A slight overexposure would whiten the skin and soften the image, giving a warmer, more diffuse aura to the body and a greater depth of field and detail to the surrounding area. While he prepared the lenses he noticed something moving at the far end of the room. What he had thought was yet another statue when he came in turned out to be a woman in black with her face covered by a veil. It was Doña Eulalia, the princess's mother, who was sobbing quietly as she crept around the room like a lost soul. She approached the dead girl and stroked her cheek.

'My angel speaks to me,' she told Sentís. 'Can't you hear her?'

Sentís nodded and continued with his preparations. The

sooner he got out of there, the better. When he was ready to start taking the first images, the photographer asked the mother to move out of the camera's field of vision for a few moments. She kissed the corpse on the forehead and stood behind the camera.

Sentís was concentrating so hard on his task he hadn't noticed that Laia had stepped into the room and was standing next to him, petrified, staring at the dead girl laid out on the bed. Before he was able to react, Señora Pons walked over to Laia and knelt down in front of her. 'Hello, sweetheart,' she said. 'Are you my angel?' The lady of the house took Sentís's daughter in her arms and pressed her against her chest. Sentís felt his blood freeze. The mother of the deceased child was singing a lullaby to Laia as she rocked her in her arms, telling her that she was her angel and they would never again be parted. At that moment Don Federico appeared. He pulled the girl from his wife's arms and led Doña Eulalia out of the room, while she begged to be left with her angel, her arms extended towards Laia. As soon as they were left alone, the photographer exposed the plates as fast as he could and put away his equipment. On his way out, Don Federico was waiting for him in the entrance hall, holding the payment for his services in an envelope. Sentís noticed that the envelope contained twice the amount they had agreed upon. Don Federico was looking at him with a mixture of hope and disdain. He made him an offer then and there: in exchange for a generous sum of money the photographer would bring his daughter to the mansion the following day and leave her there until the evening. Stupefied, Sentís looked at his daughter and then at Pons. The industrialist doubled the amount he'd offered. Sentís silently shook his head. 'Think about it,' was all Pons said when he bid him goodbye.

The photographer spent a sleepless night. Laia found him crying in the pale light of the studio and held his hand. She told him to take her to that house: she would be the angel and would play with the lady. By mid-morning they were both standing outside the mansion's gates. Sentís was handed the money by a servant and told to return at seven o'clock in the evening. He saw Laia disappear inside the large house and he dragged himself down the avenue until he found a café at the top of Calle Balmes where they served him a glass of brandy, and then another, and a further one, and as many as were necessary until it was time for him to go and pick up his daughter.

Laia spent that day playing with Doña Eulalia and the dolls that had belonged to the deceased. Doña Eulalia dressed her in the dead girl's clothes, kissed her and held her in her arms, telling her stories and talking to her about the girl's brothers, about her aunt, about a cat they'd once had but had run away. They played hide-and-seek and went up to the attic. They ran around the garden and had a snack by the fountain, throwing breadcrumbs to the coloured fish that darted through the water of the pond. At sunset, Doña Eulalia lay down on her bed with Laia by her side and drank her glass of water with laudanum. And so, embracing in the dark, the two fell asleep until one of the male servants woke Laia up and took her to the front door where her father was waiting, his eyes reddened with shame. When he saw her he fell on his knees and hugged her. The servant handed him an envelope with the money and instructed him to bring his daughter back the following day at the same time.

Every day of that week Laia went to the mansion to become the little angel, to play with her toys and wear her clothes, to answer to her name and disappear into the shadow of the dead girl who haunted every corner of that dark, sad house. By the sixth day, Laia's memories were those of little Margarita, and her past existence had evaporated. She had become that longed-for presence and had learned to embody it with more intensity than the deceased herself. She had learned to interpret looks and longings, to hear the trembling of hearts broken with loss and find the gestures and the touch that consoled the inconsolable. Without realising, she'd learned to become another person, to be nothing and nobody, to live in the skin of others. She never asked her father not to take her to that place, nor did she tell him what happened during the long hours she spent inside. The photographer, intoxicated with money and relief, salved his conscience by telling himself that this was an act of charity and Christian piety. 'If you don't want to, you don't have to go to that house any more, do you hear me?' her father would say every night when they came back from the mansion. 'But we're doing a good deed.'

The little angel disappeared on the seventh day. They said that Doña Eulalia had woken up at dawn and when she didn't find the girl next to her she had begun searching frantically for her all over the house, thinking they were still playing hide-and-seek. The laudanum and the darkness led her to the garden where she thought she heard a voice and then thought she could see a little angel – its face lined with blue veins, its lips black with poison – looking at her from the depths of the pond, calling her, inviting her to submerge herself and accept the frozen, silent embrace of the shadow that was pulling at her and whispering: 'Mother, now we'll always be together, just as you wanted.'

For years the photographer and his daughter travelled to every city and town in the country with their circus act of deceptions and pleasures. By the time she was seventeen Laia had learned to embody lives and faces aided by a few sheets of paper, an old photograph, a forgotten story or a handful of memories that refused to die. Sometimes her art served to bring back the longing of a first secret and forbidden love, and her trembling body would awaken beneath the hands of older lovers, individuals who had been able to buy everything in life except what they most desired and had allowed to slip away.

Businessmen endowed with too much money and too little life would imagine themselves, perhaps for only a few minutes, in bed with women whom the girl had conjured up from a secret longing, from the pages of a diary or a family portrait – and whose memory would stay with them the rest of their lives. Sometimes the miracle of her artistry achieved such perfection that the client forgot it was all a fantasy with which to cloud his senses and poison them with pleasure for a few moments. The client then believed the young girl was who she was pretending to be, that the object of his desire had come alive, and he did not want to let it go. He was prepared to lose his fortune or the empty, barren life he'd lugged behind him until then in order to live the rest of his dream in the arms of that girl who could become what one most desired.

When this happened – and it had been happening more and more frequently because Laia had learned to read the souls and the desires of men with such precision that even her father sometimes felt the game had gone too far – they would both run away like fugitives at dawn and hide in another city, in other streets, for weeks on end. Then Laia would spend the day hidden in the suite of a luxury hotel, sleeping most of the day, buried in a lethargy of silence and sadness, while her father did the rounds of the city's casinos and lost, in just a few days, the fortune they had accrued. Her father's promises of abandoning that life would be broken again: he would hug her and whisper that there would only be one more time, one more client, and then they would retire to a house by a lake where Laia would never again have to give life to the secret desires of some wealthy gentleman sick with loneliness. Laia knew that her father lied without realising he was lying, as all great liars do who first lie to themselves and are then unable to see the truth even if it's stabbing them in their hearts. She knew he was lying and she forgave him because she loved him and because, deep down, she wanted the game to continue, she wanted to find another character whose life she could awaken and with whom she could fill, for a few hours at least, that huge void that was growing inside her and was eating her alive at night as she waited, between silk sheets, in the suite of some grand hotel, for her father to return, inebriated with liquor and failure.

Once a month Laia received the visit of an older man wearing a dejected expression, whom her father liked to call Doctor Sentís. The doctor, a fragile person who tried to hide a look of despair and defeat behind his glasses, had seen better days. When he was young, in more affluent times, Doctor Sentís had owned a prestigious surgery on Calle Ausias March, visited by damsels of a marriageable age and dames who were more prone to reminisce. In that surgery, legs open and spread out in the blue-ceilinged room, the cream of Barcelona's bourgeoisie had no secrets or modesty before the kind doctor. His hands had delivered hundreds of children from wealthy homes and his care and advice had saved the lives and often the reputation of patients who had been deliberately kept ignorant about an important part of their bodies, the part that most burned and throbbed, so that it held more secrets for them than the mystery of the Holy Trinity.

Doctor Sentís had the quiet manners and the friendly and reassuring disposition of someone who sees no shame or embarrassment in the facts of life. Calm and affable, he knew how to gain the trust and appreciation of women and young girls, once terrorised by nuns and friars who only touched their private parts in the dark and at the devil's bidding. He would explain, with no awkwardness or fuss of any sort, how their bodies worked, and taught them not to feel bashful about what, according to him, was only the work of God. Naturally, a talented, successful man who was also decent and honest could not last long in good society, and sooner rather than later, his moment came. The fall of the righteous is always brought about by people who are most indebted to them. One doesn't betray those who want to ruin us but those who offer us a hand, even if only because we don't wish to acknowledge the debt of gratitude we owe them.

In the case of Doctor Sentís, betrayal had been in the offing for some time. For years the kind doctor had attended a lady of noble pedigree who journeyed through a marriage – lacking in contact and even words – to a man she barely knew and with whom she had shared a bed twice in twenty years. Out of habit, the lady had learned to live with cobwebs round her heart, but she refused to smother the fire between her legs, and in a city where so many gentlemen liked to treat their own wives as saints and virgins, and those of others as sluts and whores, it was easy enough for her to find lovers and fleeting devotees with whom to kill the tedium and remind herself that she was still alive, even if only from the neck down. Adventures and misadventures in others' beds carried their risks and the lady kept no secrets from the good doctor, who made sure that her pale, longing thighs did not fall prey to diseases and disreputable ailments. The doctor's potions, ointments and wise advice had kept the lady in a state of immaculate ardour for years.

As life would have it – and it usually does, given a chance – the doctor's good turns were repaid with bile and spite. Any city's polite society is a world as small as its reserves of honesty, and it was a foregone conclusion that the accursed day would come when one of those half-hour lovers, out of meanness or spite, or better still, out of self-interest, would reveal the secret and passionate life of a sad and lonely woman to the sharp eyes of her companions in jealousy. The story of the whore in silk stockings, a nickname with which some gossip-monger with literary pretensions christened her, spread like wildfire among the chattering members of a community that thrived on slander and suspicions.

Distinguished gentlemen guffawed as they described, in spiteful detail, the charms of the lady-turned-whore in silk stockings, and their no less distinguished and disdained wives spoke under their breath about how that fallen hooker, who had once been considered their friend, had performed unmentionable acts and corrupted the souls and the nether regions of their husbands and sons on all fours and with her mouth full, performing linguistic acrobatics they hadn't learned in their eleven years at the School of the Sacred Heart. The story, which was on everyone's lips and had grown increasingly outlandish, did not take long to reach the august husband of the so-called whore in silk stockings. Later, people said that nobody was to blame, that it was the lady's own decision to leave the family home, abandon her clothes and jewels and move into a cold apartment on Calle Mallorca, a place with no light and no furniture. And there, one January day, she lay down on the bed facing an open window and drank half a glassful of laudanum, until her heart stopped and her eyes, open to the icy wind of winter, shattered in the frost.

They found her naked, in the company of only a long letter – the ink not yet dry – in which she confessed her story, blaming everything on Doctor Sentís, who had confused her with his potions and his crafty words into adopting a life of abandon and lust from which only prayer and the encounter with the Lord at the doors of Purgatory could save her.

The letter, in facsimile copies or in spoken accounts, circulated widely among respectable people and in a matter of weeks the appointment book in Doctor Sentís's surgery was empty, and his quiet, calm expression had turned into that of a pariah who is barely offered a word or a look. After months of utter destitution, the doctor tried to find work in the city's hospitals. But none of them would accept him because the husband of the deceased, who had gone from being a whore in silk stockings to a saintly martyr dressed in white, was a man of great influence and had ordered and threatened that anyone who offered Doctor Sentís an opening would join him in the land of the forgotten.

With the help of time and invisibility, the kind doctor descended from the cotton-wool clouds of wealthy Barcelona and went on to live in the endless basement of its streets, where hundreds of whores with no silk stockings and other deprived souls welcomed his services and his honesty, if not with money, which they barely had, then with respect and gratitude. The kind doctor, who had been obliged to sell off his surgery on Calle Ausias March and his villa in the San Gervasio neighbourhood to survive during those difficult years, bought a modest flat on Calle Condal, where he would die many years later, happy and tired, with no regrets.

It was during those first years, when Doctor Sentís did the rounds of brothels and rooms for hire in the Raval quarter, armed with medication and common sense, that he came across the photographer, who tried to lend him his daughter's talents, free of charge. The photographer had heard how the doctor had lost his fourteen-year-old daughter, whose name was Laia, and how his wife had abandoned him shortly afterwards, unable to bear the loss they shared. Those who knew the doctor said he was haunted by the tragic death of his daughter, for he'd been unable to save her despite all his efforts. The photographer, whom the doctor had cured of an ear infection that had almost cost him his hearing and his sanity, wanted to pay him back in kind, and was convinced that, if his daughter could study photographs and tokens the doctor kept of his own dead daughter, she would be able to bring her back to life and return to him what he had most loved in the world, even if only for a few minutes. Doctor Sentís declined the offer, but struck up a friendship with the photographer and ended up becoming his daughter's doctor, visiting her once a month and keeping her safe from diseases and ailments common to her profession.

Laia adored the doctor and longed for his visits. He was the only man she knew who didn't look at her with desire, or project barren fantasies onto her. She could talk to him about things she would never have mentioned to her father and speak to him in confidence about her fears and anxieties. The doctor, who never judged his patients or the occupations life had chosen for them, couldn't hide his distaste for the way the photographer was selling the best years of his daughter's life. Sometimes he would talk to Laia about the daughter he had lost, and without anyone having to tell her, she knew she was the only person in whom the doctor confided his secrets and memories. Privately, she wished she could take the place of the other Laia, become the daughter of that sad, benevolent man, and abandon the photographer – whom greed and lies had turned into a stranger walking in her father's clothes. Death would grant her what life had denied her.

*

Not long after her seventeenth birthday, Laia knew she was pregnant. The father could have been any of the customers who, at a rate of three a week, supported the photographer's gambling debts. At first Laia hid her pregnancy from her father and made up a thousand excuses to avoid Doctor Sentís's visits during the first few months. Corsets and the art of making others only see in her what they wished to see did the rest. By the fourth month, one of her customers, a doctor who had been Doctor Sentís's rival and had now inherited a large part of his patients, became aware of her situation during a game in which Laia, wearing restraining cuffs on hands and feet, was made to undergo a cruel medical examination by the doctor, a man who was aroused by his patients' cries of pain. He left her bleeding, naked and handcuffed on the bed, where her father found her hours later.

When he discovered the truth, the photographer panicked and rushed his daughter to see a woman who practised forbidden arts in a basement on Calle Aviñón, where he asked her to get rid of the noble bastard Laia carried inside her. Surrounded by candles and buckets of smelly water, lying on a dirty, blood-stained, makeshift bed, Laia told the old witch that she was afraid and didn't want to hurt the innocent child she carried in her womb. At a nod from the photographer, the witch gave her a thick, greenish liquid to drink, which clouded her understanding and removed her willpower. She felt her father holding her wrists and the witch opening her thighs. She felt something cold and metallic making its way inside her like a tongue of ice. In her delirium, she thought she could hear the cries of a baby twisting inside her, begging her to let it live. It was then that the explosion of pain – like a thousand blades gnawing her insides, like fire blazing within – overpowered her and made her lose consciousness. The last thing she remembered was sinking into a well of steaming black blood and something, or someone, pulling her legs.

She woke up on the same dirty old bed, under the indifferent gaze of the witch. She felt weak. A dull, burning pain ravaged her lower abdomen and thighs, as if her entire body were a raw scar. Her feverish eyes met the witch's. She asked after her father. The witch shook her head in silence. Laia lost consciousness again and the next time she opened her eyes she knew dawn was breaking because of the light filtering through a tiny window that looked out at street level. The witch was standing with her back to her, preparing some concoction that smelled of honey and alcohol. Laia asked after her father. The woman handed her a hot cup and told her to drink. It would make her feel better, she said. She drank, and the warm, gelatinous balm slightly eased the gnawing agony inside her.

'Where's my father?'

'Was that your father?' asked the witch with a bitter smile.

The photographer had abandoned her, thinking she was dead. Her heart had stopped beating for two minutes, the witch explained. When he saw her lying there, dead, her father had made a run for it.

'I also thought you were dead. But a couple of minutes later you opened your eyes and started breathing again. Count yourself lucky, kid. Someone up there must love you a lot, because you've been reborn.'

When Laia had gathered enough strength to stand up and walk over to the Hotel Colón, in whose rooms they'd lived for the past three weeks, the receptionist informed her that the photographer had left the day before without leaving an address. He had taken all her clothes. The only thing he'd left behind was Laia's photograph album.

'Didn't he leave a note for me?'

'No, miss.'

Laia spent a week searching for him all over the city. Nobody had seen him recently in the casinos and cafés where he was a regular customer, but they all reminded her to tell him, if she saw him, to come and settle his outstanding debts and bills. By the second week she knew she'd never see him again. With no home and no friends, Laia went to see Doctor Sentís, who realised, the moment he saw her, that there was something wrong, and insisted on examining her. When the kind doctor discovered the damage the old witch had caused to Laia's insides, he wept inconsolably. That day he recovered a daughter and, for the first time, Laia found a father.

They lived together in the doctor's modest flat on Calle Condal. The doctor's income was minimal but enough to enrol Laia in a school for young ladies and keep up the fantasy that all would be fine for the coming year. His advanced age and the occasional carelessness in the doses of ether he secretly took to ease the pain of his existence had affected him. His hands had begun to shake and he was losing his eyesight. The man was fading and Laia left her school to look after him.

As he lost his sight, the kind doctor also began to lose awareness of reality and to believe that she was his real daughter who had come back from the dead to take care of him. Sometimes, when she held him in her arms and let him cry, Laia also believed it. When his small savings had run out, Laia was forced to unearth her arts and go back to the fray.

Now that she was free of her father's constraints, Laia discovered that her powers had increased. In just a few months the best establishments in town were fighting for her services. She limited herself to one client a month, at the highest price. For weeks she would study the case and create the persona in the fantasy she was going to embody for a few hours. She never saw the same client twice. She never revealed her real identity.

Word got round the neighbourhood that the old man was living with a stunningly beautiful young woman, and after years of abandonment his resentful wife resurfaced out of the shadows. She returned home to ruin the old age of a man who could no longer see or remember, and whose only reality was the company of a young girl whom he believed to be his dead daughter, a girl who read him books and held him in her arms, calling him, and considering him to be, her father. With the help of judges and policemen, Señora Sentís managed to throw Laia out of the house and, almost, out of the doctor's life. Laia found shelter in an institution run by an old bedroom professional, Simone de Sagnier, and spent a few years trying to forget who she was, trying to forget that her only way of feeling alive was by giving life to others. When his wife allowed her, Laia would go to the doctor's flat on Calle Condal to fetch him and take him out for a stroll. They went to places and gardens he remembered having enjoyed with his daughter and there Laia, the Laia he remembered, read books to him or brought back memories which she had not lived but had made her own. Almost three years went by like this, with old Doctor Sentís fading away week after week, until that rainy day when I followed her to the doctor's home and Laia was given the news that her father, the only father she had ever known, had died that night with her name on his lips.

ROSE OF FIRE

Translated by Lucia Graves

And so, when 23 April came round, the prisoners in the block turned to David Martín, who lay in the shadows of his cell with his eyes closed, and begged him to tell them a story with which to alleviate their tedium. 'I'll tell you a story,' he replied. 'A story about books, dragons and roses, as befits the date,[1] but above all, a story about shadows and ashes, as befits the times . . .'

(from the lost fragments of *The Prisoner of Heaven*)

---

[1] 23 April, St George's Day (World Book Day), is celebrated in Catalonia with gifts of roses and books.

I

The chronicles tell us that when the maker of labyrinths reached Barcelona on board a vessel hailing from the East, he already carried with him the germ of a curse that was to stain the city's skies with fire and blood. It was the year of Our Lord 1454. A plague had decimated the population during the winter and the city lay under a blanket of ochre-coloured smoke that rose from bonfires ablaze with hundreds of corpses and shrouds. From afar one could see the noxious pall spiralling upwards. It crept through towers and palaces and soared like an omen of death, warning travellers to continue on their way and not approach the city walls. The Holy Office had ordered the city to be sealed off and had carried out an investigation. After days of brutal interrogation it was established without a shadow of a doubt that the plague had originated in a well close to the Jewish quarter, also known as the Call de Sanaüja, where Semitic moneylenders had conjured up a demonic plot to poison its waters. The usurers' substantial goods were seized and what was left of their bodies was cast into a pit in the marshes. Now, all that anyone could do was hope that the prayers of honest citizens might bring God's blessing back to Barcelona. Every day fewer people died and more people believed that the worst was over. However, as fate would have it, the former turned out to be the fortunate ones and the latter would soon envy them for having already left that vale of misery. By the time a timid voice dared to suggest that a terrible punishment might fall upon them from Heaven to purge the vile act committed against the Jewish traders *in nomine Dei*, it was too late. Nothing fell from Heaven except ash and dust. Evil, for once, arrived by sea.

2

The ship was sighted at dawn. Some fishermen, mending their nets by the sea wall, saw it emerging out of the mist, carried in by the swell. When the prow ran aground on the shore and the hull listed to port, the fishermen clambered aboard. A powerful stench rose from the bowels of the ship: the hold was flooded and a dozen sarcophagi floated among the debris. Edmond de Luna, maker of labyrinths and sole survivor of the voyage, was found tied to the helm and burnt by the sun. At first they thought he was dead, but when they took a closer look they noticed that his wrists were still bleeding where they were tied and a cold breath issued from his lips. He carried a leather-bound notebook under his belt but none of the fishermen was able to lay his hands on it because by then a group of soldiers had turned up in the port and their captain, following instructions from the Bishop's Palace – which had been alerted to the ship's arrival – ordered the dying man to be taken to the neighbouring Hospital de Santa Marta. The captain then posted his men around the shipwreck to guard it until representatives of the Holy Office were able to inspect the vessel and make a proper Christian appraisal of the events. Edmond de Luna's notebook was handed over to the Grand Inquisitor Jorge de León, a brilliant and ambitious defender of the Church who trusted that his efforts to cleanse the world of sin would soon earn him the titles of Blessed, Saint and Beacon of the Christian Faith. After a brief inspection, Jorge de León concluded that the notebook had been written in a language unbeknown to Christianity and he ordered his men to go and find a printer named Raimundo de Sempere. Sempere had a modest workshop next to the gate of Santa Ana and, because he had travelled during his youth, knew more languages than it was prudent for a good Christian to know. Under threat of torture, Sempere the printer was made to swear he would keep the secret of what was revealed to him. Only then was he allowed to inspect the notebook, in a heavily guarded room above the library of the archdeacon's house, next to the cathedral. Jorge de León watched over him avidly.

'I think the text is written in Persian, your Holiness,' murmured a terrified Sempere.

'I'm not a saint yet,' clarified the Inquisitor. 'All in good time. Continue . . .'

And so it was that the printer spent the entire night reading and translating for the Grand Inquisitor the secret diary of Edmond de Luna, adventurer and bearer of the curse that was to bring the beast to Barcelona.

3

Thirty years earlier, Edmond de Luna had set sail from Barcelona, bound for the East, in search of wonders and adventures. His sea voyage had taken him to forbidden islands that did not appear on navigation charts, to lie with princesses and creatures of an unmentionable nature, to learn secrets of civilisations buried by time and to initiate himself in the science and art of building labyrinths, a talent that would make him famous and provide him with employment and fortune at the service of sultans and emperors. As the years went by, the accumulation of pleasure and wealth no longer meant anything to him. He had satisfied greed and ambition beyond the dreams of any mortal, and upon reaching maturity, aware that he was fast approaching the twilight of his life, he told himself that he would never again offer his services to anyone unless it were in exchange for the greatest of rewards: forbidden knowledge. For years he refused invitations to build the most prodigious and intricate labyrinths because nothing offered in payment seemed desirable to him. He thought there could be no treasure in the world that had not already been presented to him, when news came that the Emperor of the city of Constantinople required his services, for which he was prepared to reward him with a thousand-year-old secret to which no living soul had been privy for centuries. Bored, and tempted by a last opportunity to revive the flame of his soul, Edmond de Luna visited Emperor Constantine in his palace. Constantine was utterly convinced that sooner or later the siege of the Ottoman sultans would bring his empire to an end and all the knowledge that the city of Constantinople had built up over the centuries would be banished from the face of the earth. He therefore wanted Edmond to plan the greatest labyrinth ever created, a secret library, a city of books hidden beneath the catacombs of the cathedral of Hagia Sophia, where forbidden works and the prodigies of centuries of thoughts could be preserved for ever. In exchange, Emperor Constantine offered Edmond no treasure, but only a flask: a small cut-glass phial containing a scarlet liquid that shone in the dark. Constantine smiled strangely as he showed Edmond the bottle.

'I've waited many years to find a man worthy of this gift,' the Emperor explained. 'In the wrong hands, this could be an instrument for evil.'

Fascinated and intrigued, Edmond examined the bottle.

'It's a drop of blood from the last dragon,' murmured the Emperor. 'The secret of immortality.'

4

For months on end Edmond de Luna worked on the project for the great labyrinth of the books, making and remaking the plans, never satisfied with them. By then he had realised that he no longer cared about the payment, for his immortality would be secured by that prodigious library and not by some legendary magic elixir. The Emperor, patient but concerned, kept reminding him that the final siege of the Ottomans was drawing nigh and there was no time to waste. When, at long last, Edmond de Luna solved the mighty conundrum, it was too late: the troops of Mehmed II the Conqueror had besieged Constantinople. The end of the city and of the empire was imminent. The Emperor marvelled when he received the plans, but realised that he would never be able to build the labyrinth under the city that bore his name. So he asked Edmond to try to escape the siege together with so many other artists and thinkers who were about to set off for Italy.

'Dear friend,' he said, 'I know you will find the perfect place to build the labyrinth.'

In gratitude, the Emperor handed him the phial with the blood of the last dragon, but a shadow of concern clouded his face as he did so.

'When I offered you this gift, I was appealing to your avid mind, to tempt you, dear friend. I now want you also to accept this humble amulet, which one day will appeal to the wisdom of your soul if the price of ambition is too high . . .'

The Emperor removed a medal that hung round his neck and handed it to him. The pendant contained neither gold nor jewels, just a small stone that looked like a simple grain of sand.

'The man who gave it to me told me it was a tear shed by Christ.' Edmond frowned. 'I know you're not a man of faith, Edmond, but faith is found when one isn't looking for it and the day will come when your heart, and not your mind, will long for the purification of the soul.'

Edmond did not wish to contradict the Emperor so he hung the insignificant medal round his neck. With no more baggage than the plan for his labyrinth and the scarlet flask, he departed that very night. Constantinople and the empire would fall shortly afterwards, following a bloody siege, while Edmond traversed the Mediterranean in search of the city he had left in his youth.

He sailed with a group of mercenaries who had offered him passage, taking him to be a rich merchant whose pouch they could empty once they attained the high seas. When they discovered that he carried no riches upon him they decided to throw him overboard, but Edmond persuaded them to let him stay by narrating some of his adventures in the manner of Scheherazade. The trick consisted in always leaving them craving for another morsel, as a wise dweller of Damascus had once taught him. 'They will despise you for it, but they will want you even more.'

In his spare time he began to record his experiences in a notebook and in order to keep it from the prying eyes of those pirates, he wrote in Persian, an extraordinary tongue he had learned during the years he had spent in ancient Babylon. Halfway through the journey they came across a ship that was sailing adrift with no voyagers or crew. It carried large ampho-rae of wine which they took aboard and with which the pirates got drunk every night while listening to the stories recounted by Edmond – who was not allowed to taste a single drop of it. After a few days the crew began to fall ill and soon one after the other the mercenaries died, poisoned by the stolen wine.

Edmond, the only survivor, placed them one by one in sar-cophagi the pirates carried in the ship's hold – the bounty from one of their pillages. Only when he was the last man left alive on the ship and feared he might die adrift on the high seas in the most terrible solitude did he dare open the scarlet bottle and sniff its contents for a second. An instant sufficed for him to glimpse the chasm that threatened to take possession of him. He felt the vapour creeping up from the phial over his skin and for a moment saw his hands being covered in scales and his nails turning into claws, sharper and deadlier than the most fearsome sword. He then clutched the humble grain of sand hanging round his neck and prayed for his salvation to a Christ in whom he did not believe. The dark abyss of the soul faded away and Edmond breathed anew, seeing his hands becoming normal human hands again. He closed the bottle and cursed himself for being so naïve, realising then that the Emperor had not lied to him. He also knew that this was no payment or blessing of any sort. It was the key to hell.

5

When Sempere had finished translating the notebook, the first light of dawn peered through the clouds. Shortly afterwards the Inquisitor, without uttering a word, left the room and two sentries came in to fetch Sempere and lead him to a cell from which he felt sure he would never emerge alive.

While Sempere was being flung into the dungeon, the Grand Inquisitor's men were sent to the ship's hulk where, hidden in a metal coffer, they were to find the scarlet phial. Jorge de León was waiting for them in the cathedral. They had not managed to find the medal with the supposed tear of Christ to which Edmond's text referred, but the Inquisitor was unconcerned because he felt that his soul did not need any cleansing. With his eyes poisoned by greed, the Inquisitor grabbed the scarlet bottle, raised it above the altar to bless it and, thanking God and hell for that gift, downed the contents in a single gulp. A few seconds went by and nothing happened. Then the Inquisitor began to laugh. The soldiers looked at one another, disconcerted, wondering whether Jorge de León had lost his mind. For most of them this was the last thought of their lives. They saw the Inquisitor fall to his knees as a gust of icy wind swept through the cathedral, dragging with it the wooden benches, knocking down statues and lighted candles.

Then they heard his skin and his limbs cracking, and amid agonising howls Jorge de León's voice was lost in the roar of the beast emerging from his flesh, rapidly growing into a bloody tangle of scales, claws and wings. A tail punctuated by sharp edges, like the blades of an axe, fanned out like a gigantic snake and when the beast turned and showed them its face lined with fangs, its eyes alight with fire, the soldiers had no courage left to turn and run. The flames caught them as they stood there, rooted to the ground. It tore the flesh off their bones like a hurricane tearing leaves off a tree. The beast then spread its wings and the Inquisitor, saint and dragon all in one, took flight, passing through the cathedral's large rose window in a storm of glass and fire, then rising over the roofs of Barcelona.

6

For seven days and seven nights the beast sowed panic, knocking down churches and palaces, setting fire to hundreds of buildings and dismembering with its claws the trembling figures it found begging for mercy under the roofs it ripped off. Every day the scarlet dragon grew, devouring all it found in its path. Torn bodies rained down from the sky and flames from the beast's breath flowed down the streets like a torrent of blood.

On the seventh day, when everyone thought the beast was about to raze the city and kill all its inhabitants, a lone figure came out to meet it. Barely recovered, Edmond de Luna limped up the staircase leading to the very top of the cathedral. There he waited for the dragon to catch sight of him. The beast emerged from black clouds of smoke and embers, flying low, close to the roofs of Barcelona. It had grown so much that it was now larger than the church from which it had sprung.

Edmond de Luna could see himself reflected in those eyes that resembled huge pools of blood. Flying like a cannonball over the city, tearing off terrace roofs and towers, the beast opened its jaws to snap him up. Edmond de Luna then pulled out that miserable grain of sand hanging round his neck and pressed it in his fist. He recalled the words of Constantine and told himself that faith had at last found him and that his death was a very small price to pay to purify the black soul of the beast, which was none other than the soul of all men. Raising the fist that held the tear of Christ, Edmond closed his eyes and offered himself up. In a flash, the jaws swallowed him and the dragon rose high above the clouds.

Those who remember that day say that the heavens split in two and a great brightness lit up the firmament. The beast was enveloped in the flames that poured out through its teeth and as it flapped its wings it formed a huge rose of fire that covered the entire city. Silence ensued and when they opened their eyes again, the sky was shrouded as in the darkest of nights and a gentle rain of bright ash flakes was falling from on high, covering the streets, the burned ruins and the entire city of tombs, churches and palaces with a white mantle that melted when one touched it and smelled of fire and damnation.

7

That night Raimundo de Sempere managed to escape from his cell and return to his home to discover that his family and his book-printing workshop had survived the catastrophe. At dawn, the printer approached the Sea Wall. Debris from the shipwreck that had brought Edmond de Luna to Barcelona swayed on the water. The sea had begun to break up the hull and Sempere was able to enter it, as one would enter a house with a wall removed. Walking through the bowels of the ship in the ghostly light of dawn, the printer at last found what he was looking for. Salt residue had partly erased the outlines, but the plans for the great labyrinth of books were still intact, just as Edmond de Luna had conceived it. Sempere sat on the sand and unfolded the plans. His mind could not encompass the complexity and the arithmetic holding that marvel together, but he told himself that there would be other illustrious minds capable of understanding its secrets. Until then, until the time when other men wiser than him found the means of saving the labyrinth and remembering the price exacted by the beast, he would keep the plans in the family chest where some day, he had no doubt, they would find the maker of labyrinths worthy of such a challenge.

THE PRINCE OF
PARNASSUS

Translated by Lucia Graves

A bloodstained sun was sinking below the line of the horizon when Antoni de Sempere, the gentleman whom everyone called *the maker of books*, climbed up to the very top of the walls that sealed the city and sighted the cortege approaching in the distance. It was the year of Our Lord 1616 and a mist that smelled of gunpowder snaked over the rooftops of a Barcelona made of stone and dust. The maker of books turned to look at the city and his gaze became lost in the mirage of towers, palaces and narrow streets throbbing in the miasma of a perpetual darkness that was barely broken by torches and by carriages crawling along close to the walls.

'One day the walls will fall and Barcelona will spread beneath the sky like a teardrop of ink over holy water.'

The maker of books smiled as he remembered those words, spoken by his good friend when he left the city six years earlier.

'I'm taking with me its memory, for I am bound by the beauty of its streets and indebted to its dark soul, to which I vow I will return to offer my own soul and seek the embrace of its sweetest oblivion.'

The echo of hoofs approaching the city walls rescued him from his daydreaming. The maker of books turned to the east and caught sight of the cortege, already on the road leading to the large gate of San Antonio. The black hearse, escorted by two horsemen, was adorned with carved reliefs and figures winding

67

round a glass frame that was veiled with velvet curtains. Four steeds, decorated with plumes and other funeral finery, pulled the hearse, and the turning wheels raised a cloud of dust in the amber of sunset. The coachman, his face covered, could be seen on the driver's seat and behind him, crowning the hearse like a figurehead, rose the silhouette of a silver angel.

The maker of books lowered his eyes and sighed dolefully. All of a sudden, he knew he was not alone and did not even have to turn his head to verify the presence of the gentleman standing next to him. He could feel that gust of cold air and that perfume of dry flowers that always accompanied him.

'They say a good friend is one who knows how to remember as well as how to forget,' said the gentleman. 'I see you have not forgotten the meeting, Sempere.'

'Nor have you forgotten the debt, *Signore.*'

The gentleman came closer until his pale face was but a handspan away from the maker of books and Sempere was able to catch his own reflection in the dark mirror of those pupils that changed colour and narrowed like the eyes of a wolf at the sight of fresh blood. The gentleman had not aged a single day and wore the same formal attire. Sempere felt a shiver and a deep desire to run away, but all he did was nod politely.

'How did you find me?' he asked.

'The smell of ink gives you away, Sempere. Have you printed anything good recently? Anything you could recommend?'

The maker of books noticed the volume in the gentleman's hands.

'Mine is a modest press that cannot attract authors worthy of your taste. Besides, it would appear that the *signore* already has something to read for the evening.'

The gentleman exhibited his smile, revealing a string of sharp white teeth. The maker of books fixed his attention on the cortege, which was now reaching the city walls. He felt the gentleman's hand rest on his shoulder and clenched his teeth to stop himself from trembling.

'Don't be afraid, Sempere, my friend. The death rattles of Avellaneda[2] and that pack of envious scoundrels published by your friend Sebastián de Cormellas are as likely to reach posterity as the soul of my dear Antoni de Sempere is to enter the humble domain over which I preside. You have nothing to fear from me.'

'You said something similar to Don Miguel forty-six years ago.'

'Forty-seven. And I wasn't lying.'

The maker of books exchanged a brief glance with the gentleman and for a wistful moment thought he perceived the same huge sadness in his face as was engulfing his own heart.

'I thought this was a day of triumph for you, *Signore* Corelli,' he remarked.

'Beauty and knowledge are the only lights that shine on this miserable hovel that I am condemned to inhabit, Sempere. His loss is the greatest of my sufferings.'

Down below, the funeral cortege was passing through the gate of San Antonio. The gentleman made a sign to the printer, inviting him to lead the way.

'Come with me, Sempere. Let's welcome our good friend Don Miguel to the Barcelona he loved so much.'

And with those words, old Sempere abandoned himself to reminiscence, recalling that distant day when, not far from this very place, he'd met a young man named Miguel de Cervantes

---

2   Alonso Fernández de Avellaneda is the pseudonym used by the man who wrote his own Part II to Cervantes's *Don Quixote*.

Saavedra, whose destiny and whose memory were to become linked to his own fate and to his own name in the night of time . . .

Those were legendary times when history's only tool was the memory of what had never happened, and the only dreams life could attain were brief and fleeting. In those days, aspiring poets carried swords on their belts and rode their horses without thought or destination, dreaming of verses tinged with venom. Barcelona was then a fortified town cradled by an amphitheatre of mountains replete with bandits, a city hiding behind a wine-coloured sea riddled with light and pirates. Outside its gates thieves and villains were hanged to drive away unlawful greed, and inside its walls, filled to bursting point, traders, wise men, courtiers and *hidalgos* of every condition and vassalage fought at the behest of a labyrinth of conspiracies, monies and alchemies whose fame reached the horizons and yearnings of the known and the imagined world. It was said that kings and saints had shed their blood there, that words and knowledge found shelter in that town, and that any adventurer with a coin in his hands and a lie on his lips could taste glory, sleep with death and wake up the following dawn among tall towers and cathedrals feeling blessed and able to achieve fame and fortune.

At such a place, which never existed and whose name he was condemned to remember all the days of his life, there arrived one midsummer's night a young *hidalgo* of the pen-and-sword variety, riding an emaciated nag that could barely stand on its four legs after having galloped for several days. On its back it carried the then destitute Miguel de Cervantes Saavedra, who hailed from no place and from everywhere, and a young woman whose face, one might say, looked as if it had been stolen from the canvas of one of the great masters. And it would be rightly said, for it was later known that the young girl's name was Francesca di Parma, born and raised in the Eternal City barely nineteen springtides past.

As fate would have it, the scrawny nag, foaming at the mouth after having concluded its heroic trot, collapsed in exhaustion a few steps away from the gates of Barcelona and the two lovers – for that was their secret condition – ambled along the sands of the beach beneath a sky bleeding with stars until they came to the boundary marked by the walls and then, seeing the breath of a thousand bonfires rising skywards and tinting the night the colour of liquid copper, decided to look for lodging and shelter in that place that resembled a dark palace built on Vulcan's forge itself.

Don Miguel de Cervantes's arrival in Barcelona with his beloved Francesca was later recounted in similar but less florid words to the noted maker of books, Don Antoni de Sempere – whose workshop and home stood next to the gate of Santa Ana – by a limping young man of humble appearance, imposing nose and sharp wit named Sancho Fermín de la Torre who, aware of the needs of the new arrivals, kindly offered to be their guide in exchange for a few coins. That is how the couple found accommodation and sustenance in a sombre house twisted upon itself like a gnarled tree trunk. And that is how, thanks to Sancho's skills and the workings of chance, the maker of books became acquainted with the young Cervantes, with whom he would share a deep friendship to the end of his days.

Little do the experts know about the circumstances preceding Don Miguel de Cervantes's arrival in the city of Barcelona. Initiates in such matters report severe hardships and much suffering before that moment in the author's life and warn that many more, from battles to unfair sentences and prison, or to the virtual loss of a hand in combat lay ahead of him before he was able to enjoy a short time of peace in his waning years. Whatever the ins and outs of fate that had brought him there, from what the cheerful Sancho was able to gather, a great wrong and an even greater threat were hot on his heels.

Sancho, partial to tales of glowing romances and to religious plays of robust moral instruction, managed to deduce that the stimulus at the heart of such a hefty plot had to be the presence of that young woman of supernatural beauty and charms whose name was Francesca. Her skin was like a breath of light, her voice a sigh that set hearts racing, her eyes and lips a promise of pleasures whose description escaped the rhyming talents of poor Sancho, for the magic suggested by the shapes beneath those clothes of silk and lace was enough to alter his pulse and his reason. And so Sancho concluded that the young poet, having tasted that heavenly poison, was in all likelihood beyond salvation, for there could be no honest man on this earth who would not have sold his soul, his horse and even his mind for a moment of bliss in the arms of that siren.

'Cervantes, my friend,' Sancho asserted, 'it is not for a sad peasant like me to tell Your Excellency that a countenance and frame so magnificent will cloud the mind of any man in breathing condition, but my nose, which after my gut is my shrewdest organ, leads me to think that wherever it was that Your Honour removed that marvellous example of womanhood from, you will not be forgiven for it, and there is not enough room on earth in which to hide a Venus of such delicious substance.'

Needless to say, in pursuit of the drama and the scene-setting, the words and musicality of good Sancho's drivel have been rearranged and improved by the pen of this your humble and reliable narrator, but the essence and wisdom of his judgement remain untouched and unadulterated.

'Oh, my friend, were I to tell you . . .' sighed a mortified Cervantes.

And tell him he did, for the wine of storytelling ran through his veins and, as the heavens would have it, it was his practice to firstly tell himself the things of the world in order to understand them and then tell them to others, draped in the music and light of literature, because he sensed that if life was not a dream it was at least a pantomime where the cruel absurdity of the narrative always ran behind the scenery, and there was no greater or more effective vengeance twixt heaven and earth than to sculpt beauty and wit by dint of words if one was to find sense in the nonsense of things.

The account of how he had arrived in Barcelona, fleeing from monumental dangers, and which was the origin and nature of that prodigious creature named Francesca di Parma, was expounded by Don Miguel de Cervantes seven nights later. At Cervantes's request, Sancho had put him in touch with Antoni de Sempere, for it appears that the young poet had written a play, some sort of romance about mysterious enchantments, spells and wild passions, which he wished to see committed to paper.

'It is of extreme importance that I see my work printed before the next moon, Sancho. My life and that of Francesca depend on it.'

'How can someone's life depend on a bunch of verses and the conjunction of the moon, Master?'

'Believe me, Sancho. I know what I'm saying.'

Sancho, who secretly did not believe in any poetry or astronomy other than those promised by a fine meal and a generous tumble in the hay with some plump and cheerful lass, trusted in his patron's words and performed the necessary tasks to bring about the meeting. Leaving the beautiful Francesca in her room, fast asleep in the arms of the nymphs, the two men departed at nightfall. They had arranged to meet Sempere at an inn that lay in the shadow of the fishermen's great cathedral – known as the basilica of Santa María del Mar – and there, sitting in a corner by candlelight, all three partook of a good wine and a loaf of bread with rashers of salted pork. The clientele was made up of fishermen, pirates, murderers and sundry visionaries. Laughter, quarrels and thick clouds of smoke floated in the golden darkness of the tavern.

'Tell Don Antonio about your comedy,' Sancho encouraged the author.

'Actually, it's a tragedy,' Cervantes clarified.

'And pray, what is the difference, if the master will forgive my utter ignorance of fine lyric genres?'

'Comedy shows us that one must not take life too seriously, and tragedy teaches us what happens when we pay no attention to what comedy teaches us,' Cervantes explained.

Sancho nodded without batting an eyelid and rounded off the job with a fierce bite at his bacon.

'Isn't poetry grand?' he mumbled.

Sempere, somewhat bereft of orders in those days, listened with interest to the young poet. Cervantes carried a bundle of papers in a folder, which he showed the maker of books. The latter examined them carefully, stopping here and there to cast his eye over certain turns of phrase in the text.

'There's work here for quite a few days . . .'

Cervantes pulled a bag from his belt and dropped it on the table. A handful of coins peeped out of it. As soon as the filthy lucre shone in the candlelight, Sancho hid it with an anguished expression.

'For God's sake, Master, don't show such fine fodder around here – these places are stuffed with villains and cut-throats who would slice your gullet and ours too with just one whiff of the aroma given off from these doubloons.'

'Sancho is right, my friend,' Sempere confirmed, eyeing the crowd.

Cervantes hid the monies and sighed.

Sempere poured him another glass of wine and began examining the poet's pages in more detail. The work, described by the author as a tragedy in three acts and an epistle, was titled *A Poet in Hell* and narrated the hardships of a young Florentine artist who, accompanied by Dante's ghost, penetrates the depths of the underworld in order to rescue the soul of his beloved, the daughter of a cruel and corrupt family of nobles who had sold her to the Prince of Darkness in exchange for fame, fortune and glory in the finite, earthly world. The last scene took place inside the Duomo, where the hero had to prise the lifeless body of his chosen damsel from the claws of an angel of light and fire.

Sancho thought it sounded like some sinister puppet tale, but didn't say anything because he sensed that regarding such matters bookworms had a thin skin and didn't take any criticism easily.

'Tell me how you came to compose this work, my friend,' Sempere inquired.

Cervantes, who had already knocked back three or four glasses of wine, nodded. It was evident that he wanted to unburden himself of the secret that was weighing him down.

'Rest assured that Sancho and I will keep your secret, my friend, whatever it may be.'

Sancho raised his goblet of wine to that noble sentiment.

Cervantes hesitated. 'My story is the story of a curse,' he began.

'Like that of all apprentice poets,' said Sempere. 'Pray continue.'

'It's the story of a man in love.'

'Agreed. But fear not, such tales are highly favoured by the public,' Sempere reassured him.

Sancho nodded repeatedly.

'Love is the only creature that doesn't learn from its mistakes,' he agreed. 'And wait until you see the lass in question, Sempere,' he added, suppressing a belch. 'She's of the kind that truly lifts one's spirit.'

Cervantes stared at him censoriously.

'Please forgive me, sir,' Sancho ventured. 'It's this wicked wine that's taking hold of me. The virtue and purity of the lady plainly speak for themselves, and may the very heavens fall on my empty head if at any moment I entertained a single impure thought in this regard.'

The three men looked briefly up at the tavern's ceiling, and seeing that the Creator was not on duty and no mishap had taken place, they smiled, raised their glasses and toasted the happy occasion of their encounter. And that is how the wine, which makes men become sincere when they least need to, and gives them courage when they should hold back, persuaded Cervantes to tell the story within the story, that which fools and murderers call the truth.

A POET IN HELL

According to the proverb, a man must walk while he still has legs, speak while he still has a voice and dream while he still preserves his innocence, because sooner or later he will be unable to stand up, his breath will falter and the only dream he will long for is the eternal night of oblivion. With these words as his saddlebags, an arrest warrant out for him – because of a duel that had taken place in murky circumstances – and the fire of youth in his veins, Miguel de Cervantes departed from the town of Madrid in the year of Our Lord 1569, heading for the legendary cities of Italy in search of wonders, beauty and science which, according to those who knew them, they possessed in far greater measure and grace than any other place to be found on the maps of the kingdom. Many were the adventures and misfortunes that befell him in those lands, but the greatest of them all was his happening upon that creature of extraordinary radiance whose name was Francesca, from whose lips he tasted heaven and hell, and in whose desire he was to seal his destiny forever.

Barely nineteen, Francesca had already lost all hope in life. She was the last daughter of a despicable and destitute family who scraped together a living in an old house that leaned over the waters of the River Tiber in the ancient city of Rome. Her brothers – deceitful, malicious good-for-nothings – lazed about and committed thefts and petty crimes with which they barely managed to put a crust of bread in their mouths. Her prematurely aged parents, who insisted they had conceived her in the autumn of their unhappy lives, were just a couple of miserly swindlers who had found little Francesca crying in the still warm arms of her real mother, a nameless young girl who had died giving birth to her under the arches of the old bridge of Castel Sant'Angelo.

As they debated whether to fling the baby into the river and just take the copper medal her mother wore round her neck, the two villains noticed the child's astonishing perfection and decided to keep her, for surely such a gift would fetch a good price among the most refined and wealthy families, those providing an entry to the doors of the court. As the days, weeks and months went by, their greed intensified, for day by day the little girl showed herself to be a creature of such beauty and charm that in the minds of her captors her price and value could only rise. When she was ten, a Florentine poet who was passing through Rome noticed her one day as she went down to the river for water – not far from where she had been born and had lost her mother. Faced with the magic in her eyes, the poet dedicated a few lines to her and gave her what would be her name, Francesca, for her adoptive family had not even bothered to give her one. And so Francesca grew, until she blossomed into a woman of exquisite fragrance whose very presence stopped conversations and brought time to a halt. Only the immeasurable sadness of her eyes tarnished the picture of a beauty beyond words.

Very soon, artists from all corners of Rome began to offer enticing sums to her scheming parents to be allowed to use her as a model for their works. When they saw her they were convinced that if anyone with talent and skill were able to capture only a tenth of her enchantment on canvas or marble, he would pass into history as the greatest artist of all time. The demand for her services did not cease, and the one-time beggars now basked in the splendour of new wealth, riding about in garish carriages fit for a cardinal, dressed in coloured silks and smearing their private parts with scent to disguise the shame that covered their hearts.

When Francesca came of age, her parents, fearing they might lose the treasure that had built their fortune, decided to offer her hand in marriage. Contrary to the usual practice of providing a dowry, as was expected of the bride's family in those days, their audacity led them to request a substantial payment in exchange for granting the damsel's hand and body to the highest bidder. An unprecedented auction took place which was won by one of the most celebrated and renowned artists in the city, Don Anselmo Giordano. Giordano was by then a mature man in his declining years, with body and soul damaged by decades of excess, and a heart poisoned by greed and envy because, despite all the tributes, wealth and praise his work had garnered, his secret dream had been to surpass Leonardo in both name and reputation.

The great Leonardo had been dead for five decades, but Anselmo Giordano had never been able to forget, or forgive, the day when, still only an adolescent, he had gone to the master's workshop to offer his services as an apprentice. Leonardo examined some of the sketches he had brought with him and said a few kind words about them. Young Anselmo's father was a well-known banker to whom Leonardo owed a favour or two, and the boy was convinced that his place in the workshop of the greatest artist of the day was guaranteed. Much to his surprise, Leonardo, not without sadness, added that although he appreciated a certain talent in his lines, it was not enough to make him any different from a thousand and one aspirants like him who would never even reach mediocrity. He told him that he did have some ambition, but not enough to distinguish him from so many other apprentices who would never be capable of sacrificing what was needed to deserve the light of true inspiration. And finally, he told him that perhaps he could acquire some skill, but never enough to make it worth his while to devote his life to a profession where only geniuses managed to get by.

'Young Anselmo,' said Leonardo, 'don't let my words distress you. Consider them a blessing, for your kind father will make you a wealthy man for life, one who will not have to fight with brush and chisel for a living. You will be a fortunate man, you will be a man loved and respected by your fellow citizens, but what you will never be, even if you possessed all the gold in the world, is a genius. Few fates can be as cruel or as bitter as that of a mediocre artist who spends his life envying and cursing his rivals. Don't waste your life on an inauspicious destiny. Let art and beauty be created by others who have no choice. And in time, learn to forgive my honesty which will hurt today but tomorrow, if you accept it with good grace, will save you from your own hell.'

With these words, Master Leonardo dismissed young Anselmo, who was to wander for hours through the streets of Rome weeping tears of anger. When he returned to his father's house he announced that he did not wish to study with Leonardo, whom he considered a fraud, a producer of vulgar pieces for ignorant masses who were incapable of appreciating true art.

'I will be a pure artist, only for a select few who will be able to understand the depth of my commitment.'

His father, who was a patient man and, like all bankers, had more understanding of human nature than the wisest of cardinals, embraced him and told him to fear not, as he would never want for anything – not sustenance, or admirers, or praise for his work. Before dying, the banker made sure that it would be so.

Anselmo Giordano never forgave Leonardo, because a man can forgive everything except being told the truth. Fifty years later, his hatred and his wish to see the false master discredited were greater than ever.

When Anselmo Giordano heard the fabulous tale of young Francesca told by poets and artists, he sent his servants with a bagful of gold coins to the family's home and requested their presence. The young woman's parents, dressed like circus monkeys on a visit to the court of Mantua, turned up at Giordano's residence escorting the lass, who was clad in humble rags. When the artist's eyes rested upon Francesca his heart seemed to stop for a moment. Everything he had heard about her was true, nay, more than true. Nowhere in the world did such beauty exist – nor had it ever existed – and he knew, as only an artist can know, that her charm did not stem, as everyone believed, from that skin, or that shapely body, but from the luminosity emanating from within her, from her sad, forlorn eyes, from her lips silenced by fate.

So strong was the impression Francesca di Parma made on Master Giordano that he was convinced he must not let her escape, that he could not allow her to sit for any other painter and that such a marvel of nature must belong to him and to him alone. It was the only way he would be able to create a body of work that would earn him the people's favour over that of the contemptible and odious Leonardo. It was the only way his fame and reputation would surpass those of the deceased Leonardo, whose name he would no longer need to scorn in public, because once he had reached the pinnacle he would be the one who could permit himself to ignore him and claim that his work had only ever existed to excite the coarse and the ignorant. Then and there, Giordano made an offer that exceeded the most lavish dreams of the vile couple who called themselves Francesca's parents. The wedding was to take place a week later in the chapel of Giordano's palace. Francesca did not utter a single word during the transaction.

Seven days later, young Cervantes was ambling through town in search of inspiration, when the retinue accompanying a large golden carriage cleared the way through the crowd. The procession halted for an instant as it crossed Via del Corso, and it was then that he saw her. Francesca di Parma, wearing the most delicate silks woven by Florentine craftsmen, gazed at him in silence from the carriage window. So profound was the sadness he read in her eyes, and such was the power of that stolen spirit as it was being led to prison, that Cervantes was seized by the cold certainty that for the first time in his life he had seen the path of his true destiny in the face of an unknown woman.

As he watched the procession disappear into the distance, Cervantes asked who that creature could be, and the people walking by told him the story of Francesca di Parma. Listening to them, he recalled having heard rumours and gossip about her, but he had dismissed these, attributing them to the wild fabrications of local bards. And yet, the fable was true. Sublime beauty had become embodied in a simple, humble woman and, as could be expected, people had done nothing but ensure her misfortune and humiliation. Young Cervantes wanted to follow the procession to Giordano's palace, but he couldn't find the strength. To him, the celebrations and merrymaking sounded like some ominous music, and all he could see was a tragedy: the destruction of purity and perfection by men's greed, wickedness and ignorance.

Pressing against the crowds who wished to follow the nuptial ceremonies outside the famous artist's palace, Cervantes walked back to his inn, filled with sadness almost as great as that which he had perceived in the eyes of the mysterious young woman. That very night, while Master Giordano removed the silks draped over Francesca di Parma's body and caressed every inch of her skin with lust and incredulity, the house of the young woman's family, built on a dangerous location above the Tiber and unable to take the weight of the treasures and glittering ornaments accumulated at her expense, collapsed into the freezing waters of the river, taking with it all the members of the clan, whom nobody would ever see again.

Not far from there, a wakeful Cervantes confronted ink and paper by the light of an oil lamp, preparing to write down everything he'd witnessed that day. With a faltering hand, and lost for words, he attempted to describe the impression made on him by that brief exchange of glances with the damsel Francesca on Via del Corso. All the art he thought he possessed withered on the tip of his pen and not a single word settled on the page. He told himself that if perchance his writing could ever capture a mere tenth of the magic radiating from that presence, his name and reputation would rise among those of the greatest poets in history and he would become a king among narrators, a prince of Parnassus whose light would illuminate the lost paradise of literature and,

moreover, wipe from the earth the odious reputation of that per-
fidious playwright Lope de Vega, on whom both fortune and glory
did not cease to smile, a man who had attained unprecedented
triumphs since early youth, while he was barely able to complete a
single line of poetry that would not embarrass the paper on which
it was written. Moments later, understanding the darkness of his
desire, he felt ashamed of his vanity and of the insane envy that
was eating away at him, and he told himself that he was no better
a man than old Giordano, who at that very moment must be licking the forbidden honey with his mendacious lips and exploring,
with trembling hands reeking of infamy, the secrets he had stolen
by dint of doubloons.

In his infinite cruelty, Cervantes presumed, God had abandoned
Francesca di Parma's beauty to the hands of men to remind them
of the ugliness of their souls, the meanness of their endeavours
and the rancour of their desires.

Days passed, but the memory of that brief encounter would not
die away. Cervantes sat at his desk trying to assemble the pieces
of a drama that would satisfy the public and capture their imagination, like the ones Lope seemed to write effortlessly, but all his
mind was able to evoke was the sense of loss Francesca di Parma's image had planted in his heart. As for the play he had decided to write, his pen filled page after page of a troubled romance in
whose verses he tried to recreate the young woman's lost story.
In his account, Francesca had no memory, she was a blank page;
her character was a fate as yet untold that only he could make up,
a promise of purity that would restore his determination to believe
in something clean and innocent set in a world of lies and deceit, a
world of trickery, meanness and blame. He spent sleepless nights
hammering his imagination, pulling at the strings of his ingenuity
to the point of exhaustion and despite all that, when he reread his
folios at dawn he would toss them into the fire because he knew

they did not deserve to share the light of day with the being who had inspired them, the woman who was slowly wasting away in the prison that Giordano, whom he had never seen but already loathed with every fibre of his being, had built for her inside the walls of his palace.

The days became weeks and the weeks turned into months, and soon half a year had passed since the wedding between Anselmo Giordano and Francesca di Parma, during which time nobody in the whole of Rome had set eyes on them again. People knew that the best merchants in town delivered provisions to the palace gates and these were received by Tomaso, the master's personal servant. They knew that once a week Antonio Mercanti's workshop provided the master with canvases and other materials for his work. But not a soul could say they'd seen the artist or his young wife in person. On the day that marked six months since the nuptials, Cervantes was visiting a famous impresario who managed some of the most important theatres in the city and was always on the lookout for new authors with talent, hunger and a willingness to work for a pittance. Thanks to the recommendation of various colleagues of his, Cervantes had been granted an audience with Don Leonello, an extravagant gentleman of pompous manners and noble attire who kept on his desk a collection of glass vials containing, or so they said, the intimate secretions of great courtesans whose virtue he had deflowered. Leonello, who wore a small brooch on his lapel in the shape of an angel, kept him standing while he skimmed over the pages of his play, feigning boredom and disdain.

'*A Poet in Hell*,' murmured the impresario. 'That's been done. This story has been told by others before you, and better too. What I'm looking for, let's say, is innovation. Audacity. Vision.'

Cervantes knew from experience that people who say they look for these noble virtues in art are the ones who are normally most incapable of recognising them, but he also knew that an empty stomach and a light pocket can remove all arguments and rhetoric from the best of us. If his instinct told him anything, it was that Leonello, who wore the appearance of an old fox, did at least feel perturbed by the nature of the material he had brought to him.

'I'm sorry to have wasted Your Lordship's time—'

'Not so fast,' Leonello cut in. 'I said this is nothing new, but not that it is, let's say, excremental. You do have some talent, but you lack professional skills. And what you don't have, let's say, is taste. Or a sense of opportunity.'

'I thank you for your generosity.'

'And I you for your sarcasm, Cervantes. You Spaniards suffer from too much pride and not enough perseverance. Don't give up so soon. Learn from your compatriot Lope de Vega. A true genius – *genio y figura* as you Spaniards say.'

'I'll bear that in mind. Does Your Excellency then see any possibility of accepting my work?'

Leonello burst out laughing.

'Do pigs fly? Nobody wants to see, let's say, bleak dramas telling them that the human heart is rotten, and that hell is oneself and one's neighbour, Cervantes. People go to the theatre to laugh, to cry and to be reminded of how good and noble one is. You've not yet lost your naivety and you think you have, let's say, the truth to tell. You'll be cured of it in a few years, or at least that's what I hope, because I wouldn't like to see you burned at the stake or rotting away in a prison cell.'

'So you don't think my play could interest anybody . . .'

'That's not what I said. Let's say that I know someone who perhaps might be interested.'

Cervantes felt his pulse race.

'Hunger is so predictable,' sighed Leonello.

'Hunger, unlike Spaniards, has no pride and is brimming with perseverance,' suggested Cervantes.

'You see? You do have some training. You know how to turn a sentence around and construct, let's say, a dramatic line as a reply. It's only a beginner's effort, but plenty of louts whose plays have been performed can't even write an exit stage left . . .'

'Can you help me, then, Don Leonello? I'll do whatever it takes and I learn quickly.'

'I've no doubt about that . . .'

Leonello observed him doubtfully.

'Anything, Your Excellency. I beg you . . .'

'There *is* something that might interest you. But it entails, let's say, some risks.'

'Risks don't scare me. No more than poverty, at least.'

'In that case . . . I know a certain gentleman with whom I have, let's say, an agreement. When a promising young man with some talent, like you, let's say, comes across my path, I send him off to see him and he, let's say, is grateful. In his own way.'

'I'm all ears.'

'That's what worries me . . . It so happens that the gentleman in question is, let's say, passing through the city.'

'Is the gentleman a theatre impresario like Your Excellency?'

'Let's say he's something like that. A publisher.'

'Even better . . .'

'If you say so. He has a presence in Paris, Rome and London and he's always on the lookout for a special type of talent. Like yours, let's say . . .'

'I'm enormously grateful for—'

'Don't thank me. Go and see him and tell him I sent you. But hurry up. I know he's only in town for a few days . . .'

Leonello wrote a name down on a sheet of paper and handed it to him.

'You'll find him in the Locanda Borghese, in the evening.'

'Do you think he'll be interested in my play?'

Leonello smiled mysteriously.

'Good luck, Cervantes.'

At nightfall Cervantes put on the only clean set of clothes he possessed and walked over to the Locanda Borghese, a villa surrounded by canals and gardens, not far from Anselmo Giordano's palace. At the foot of the stairway he was startled by a discreet servant who announced that he was expected and that Andreas Corelli would receive him shortly in one of the halls. Cervantes imagined that perhaps Leonello was kinder than he portrayed himself to be and had sent a note recommending him to his publisher friend. The servant led Cervantes to a large oval library. The room lay in the shadows and was heated by a fire that cast an intense amber glow dancing over endless walls of books. Two large armchairs faced one another by the fireplace. After a moment's hesitation, Cervantes sat in one of them and was soon enveloped by the warm aura and the hypnotic dance of the flames. It took him a couple of minutes to realise that he was not alone. A tall, angular figure occupied the opposite armchair. He was dressed in black and wore a silver angel that was identical to the one he'd seen on Leonello's lapel that afternoon. What he first noticed about him were his hands, the largest he had ever seen, pale and displaying long, sharp fingers. Then he noticed his eyes: two mirrors reflecting the flames and Cervantes's own face, eyes that never blinked and seemed to alter the shape of their pupils without moving a single muscle.

'My good friend Leonello tells me you're a man of great talent, but little fortune.'

Cervantes swallowed hard.

'Don't allow my appearance to trouble you, Señor Cervantes. Appearances do not always deceive, but frequently confound.'

Cervantes nodded but said nothing. Corelli smiled, tight-lipped.

'You've brought a play to show me. Am I wrong?'

Cervantes handed him the manuscript and noticed how Corelli smiled when he saw the title.

'It's a first draft,' ventured Cervantes.

'Not any longer,' said Corelli as he leafed through it.

Cervantes watched the publisher read calmly, occasionally smiling or raising his eyebrows in surprise. A wine glass and a bottle of some fine-looking liquid seemed to have materialised on the table between the two armchairs.

'Help yourself, Cervantes. Man cannot scrape a living on writing alone.'

Cervantes poured a glass of wine and raised it to his lips. A sweet, intoxicating aroma flooded his palate. He downed the wine in three gulps and felt an irrepressible desire to help himself to some more.

'Don't be shy, my friend. A glass with no wine is an insult to life.'

Soon Cervantes had lost count of the number of glasses he'd savoured. A gratifying and comforting drowsiness had taken hold of him and through half-closed eyelids he could see that Corelli was still reading the manuscript. He heard bells striking midnight in the distance. Shortly afterwards, the curtain of a deep sleep fell and Cervantes abandoned himself to the silence.

When he opened his eyes again, Corelli's silhouette was outlined against the fire. The publisher was facing the flames, standing with his back to Cervantes and holding the manuscript in his hand. Cervantes felt a hint of nausea, the sweet aftertaste of the wine in his throat, and wondered how much time had gone by.

'One day you'll write a masterpiece, Cervantes,' said Corelli, 'But this isn't it.'

Without further ado, the publisher threw the manuscript into the fire. Cervantes leaped towards the flames but the roar of the fire stopped him. He watched helplessly as the fruit of his labours burned, as the lines of ink turned into blue flames and trails of white smoke scurried over the pages like snakes of gunpowder. Devastated, he fell on his knees and when he turned to face Corelli he saw the publisher looking at him with pity.

'Sometimes a writer must burn a thousand pages before writing a single one that deserves bearing his signature. You've barely begun. Your work awaits you on the threshold of your maturity.'

'You had no right to do that . . .'

Corelli smiled and stretched out a hand to help him up from the floor. Cervantes hesitated, but finally accepted.

'I want you to write something for me, my friend. Without haste. Even if it takes you years, and believe me, it will. It will take longer than you imagine. Something in accord with your ambition and your desires.'

'What do you know about my desires?'

'Like most aspiring poets, Cervantes, you're like an open book. For that reason, because your *Poet in Hell* seems to me simply a child's game, a bout of measles you must go through, I choose to make you a firm offer. An offer for you to write a work that will meet your high standards, and mine.'

'You've burned everything I was able to write in months of work.'

'And I've done you a favour. Now tell me, from your heart, if you really think I'm wrong.'

It took him a while, but Cervantes agreed.

'And tell me whether I'm mistaken when I say that in your heart you cherish the hope of creating a work that will eclipse that of your rivals, that will sully the name of that Señor Lope and his prolific ingenuity . . .'

Cervantes wanted to protest, but the words wouldn't reach his lips. Corelli smiled again.

'You don't need to feel ashamed about that. Or to think that such a desire turns you into someone like Giordano . . .'

Cervantes looked up disconcertedly.

'Of course I know the story of Giordano and his muse,' replied Corelli, anticipating his question. 'I know it because I've known the old master for many years, before you were even born.'

'Anselmo Giordano is a vile person.'

Corelli laughed.

'No, he's not. He's just a man.'

'A man who deserves to pay for his crimes.'

'Is that what you think? Don't tell me you're also going to fight a duel with him.'

Cervantes paled. How could the publisher know he'd left Madrid months ago fleeing from an arrest warrant issued as a consequence of a duel?

Corelli gave him a wicked smile and pointed an accusing finger at him.

'And what crimes are those you're attributing to poor Giordano, aside from his tendency to paint bucolic scenes of goats, Virgin Marys and little shepherds to suit the tastes of traders and bishops, and madonnas with ample busts to cheer up parishioners during prayer?'

'He kidnapped that poor girl and keeps her imprisoned in his palace to satisfy his greed and his baseness. To hide his lack of talent. To erase his shame.'

'How quickly men judge their fellow humans for actions that they themselves would commit if the opportunity arose . . .'

'I would never do what he has done.'

'Are you sure?'

'Completely.'

'Would you dare to be put to the test?'

'I don't understand . . .'

'Tell me, Señor Cervantes. What do you know about Francesca di Parma? And don't give me that tale about the dishonoured maiden and her cruel childhood. You've already shown me that you've mastered the rudiments of theatre . . .'

'All I know is . . . that she doesn't deserve to live in a prison.'

'Is that because of her beauty? Do you think that ennobles her?'

'Because of her purity. Because of her goodness. Her innocence.'

Corelli licked his lips.

'You're still in time to abandon literature and embrace the sacrament of priesthood, my friend Cervantes. Better pay, better lodgings, and, it goes without saying, hot and plentiful meals. One needs a great deal of faith to be a poet. More than you claim.'

'You make fun of everything.'

'Only of you, Cervantes.'

Cervantes stood up and made as if to go to the door.

'Then I'll leave Your Grace alone to laugh to your heart's content.'

Cervantes was about to reach the door when it slammed shut in his face with such force that it knocked him over. He was trying to get back on his feet when he discovered that Corelli was leaning over him, a six-foot, bony figure, looking as if he were about to fling himself upon him and tear him apart.

'Get up,' he ordered.

Cervantes obeyed. The publisher's eyes seemed to have changed. Two huge black pupils spread across them. Cervantes had never been so frightened. He took a step back and bumped into the wall of books.

'I'm going to give you one opportunity, Cervantes. An opportunity to become yourself, to stop wandering along paths that would lead you to live lives that are not your own. And as with every opportunity, the final choice will be yours. Do you accept my offer?'

Cervantes shrugged.

'This is my offer. You will write a masterpiece, but in order to do so you will have to lose what you love most. Your work will be praised, envied and imitated till the end of time, but a void will open in your heart, a void a thousand times greater than the glory and the vanity of your inventiveness, because only then will you understand the true nature of your feelings and only then will you know whether or not you are, as you now believe you are, a better man than Giordano and all those who, like him, have already fallen on their knees at the sight of their own reflection when they have accepted this challenge ... Do you accept it?'

Cervantes sought to avert Corelli's eyes.

'I can't hear you.'

'I accept it,' he heard himself say.

Corelli stretched out his hand and Cervantes shook it. The publisher's fingers closed over his like a spider and he felt the cold breath of Corelli on his face. It smelled of dug-up earth and dead flowers.

'Every Sunday, at midnight, Tomaso, Giordano's servant, opens the door to an alleyway that lies hidden among trees on the eastern side of the palace. He sets off to fetch a bottle of tonic which Avianno, the healer, prepares for him with spices and rosewater, and with which Tomaso hopes he will recover the spirit of youth. This is the only night in the week when the master's servants and guards are not at work, and the next shift doesn't commence until dawn. During the half-hour the servant is away, the door is open and nobody guards the palace ...'

'And what do you expect of me?' stammered Cervantes.

'The question is what you expect of yourself, dear sir. Is this the life you wish to live? Is this the man you wish to be?'

The flames in the fireplace flickered and went out, the shadows moved along the library walls like stains of spilt ink, enveloping Corelli. When Cervantes was about to reply, he was already alone.

That Sunday at midnight, Cervantes waited, hidden among the trees that flanked Giordano's palace. The bells had just finished striking twelve when a small side door opened and the hunched figure of the artist's old servant set off down the alley. Cervantes waited for his shadow to disappear in the night and crept towards the door. He grasped the handle and pushed. Just as Corelli had predicted, the door opened. Cervantes took one last look outside and, trusting he had not been seen, entered. As soon as the door closed behind him he realised he was surrounded by utter darkness and he cursed his lack of common sense for not having brought a candle or a lamp to guide him. He felt the walls, which were damp and slippery like the guts of a beast, and groped his way forward until he bumped into the first step of what seemed to be a spiral staircase. Slowly he ascended and soon a pale glimmer of light outlined a stone arch leading to a wide corridor. The floor of the corridor was patterned with large black and white marble squares, resembling those of a chessboard. Like a pawn advancing furtively in a move, Cervantes made his way into the imposing palace. Even before he had reached the end of that gallery he began to notice frames and canvases abandoned by the walls, or thrown on the floor and forming what looked to him like debris from a shipwreck strewn all over the abode. He walked past the entrances to rooms and halls where unfinished portraits were piled up on shelves, tables and chairs. A marble staircase leading to the upper floors was covered with broken canvases, some of them proof of the fury with which their creator had destroyed them. When he reached the central atrium, Cervantes found himself standing beneath a great beam of ethereal lunar light that filtered down from the dome crowning the palace, where pigeons fluttered about, sending the echo of their wings through dilapidated corridors and rooms. He knelt down in front of one of the portraits and recognised the blurred face on the canvas – an unfinished likeness, like all the others, of Francesca di Parma.

Cervantes looked around him and saw hundreds more like that one, all of them discarded, all of them abandoned. Then he understood why nobody had seen Master Giordano again. In his determination to recover his lost inspiration and capture the luminosity of Francesca di Parma, the artist had been losing his mind with every brushstroke. His madness had left its trace on unfinished canvases that were scattered all over the palace like the skin of a snake.

'I've been expecting you for a long time,' said a voice behind his back.

Cervantes turned around. An old, emaciated man, with long tangled hair, filthy clothes and glazed, bloodshot eyes, was watching him with a smile from a corner of the large hall. He was sitting on the floor, alone, holding a glass and a bottle of wine. Master Giordano, one of the most famous artists of his time, transformed into a mad beggar in his own home.

'You've come to take her, haven't you?' he asked. Cervantes didn't know what to reply. The old painter poured himself another glass of wine and raised a toast. 'My father built this palace for me, did you know? He said it would protect me from the world. But who can protect us from ourselves?'

'Where is Francesca?' asked Cervantes.

The painter gave him a long look, savouring the wine with a mocking expression.

'Do you really think you'll triumph where so many have failed?'

'I'm not looking for any triumph, Master. I simply wish to free a girl who does not deserve to live in a place like this.'

'A noble sentiment indeed coming from a man who even lies to himself,' Giordano declared.

'I've not come here to argue with you, Master. If you don't tell me where she is, I'll find her myself.'

Giordano downed his wine and nodded.

'And I won't be the one to stop you, young man.'

Giordano looked up at the stairway that rose through the mist towards the dome. Cervantes scanned the dark and saw her. Francesca di Parma, an apparition of light amid shadows, was descending the stairs slowly, naked and barefoot. Cervantes rushed to remove his cloak and cover her, enfolding her in his arms. The immeasurable sorrow in her eyes rested upon him.

'The gentleman must leave this accursed place while there is still time,' she murmured.

'I will leave, but in your company.'

From his corner, Giordano applauded the scene.

'Magnificent scene. The lovers at midnight on the stairway to heaven.'

Francesca looked at the old painter, the man who had held her prisoner for half a year, with tenderness and without any hint of resentment. Giordano smiled sweetly, like a lovesick youth.

'Forgive me, my love, for not having been what you deserved.'

Cervantes tried to draw the young girl away, but she kept her eyes riveted on her captor, a man who seemed close to his dying breath. Giordano filled his glass with wine again and offered it to her.

'One last farewell sip, my love.'

Letting go of Cervantes's embrace, Francesca walked over to

Giordano and knelt down beside him. She stretched out a hand and stroked his wrinkled face. The artist closed his eyes and lost himself in her touch. Before she left, Francesca accepted the glass and drank the wine he was offering her. She drank slowly, with her eyes closed, clutching the glass with both hands. Then she let it fall and it shattered into a thousand pieces at her feet. Cervantes held her and she surrendered to him. Without even a parting glance at the painter, Cervantes hastened to the main door of the palace with the girl in his arms. When he stepped outside the guards and the servants were waiting for him. Not one of them tried to stop him. One of the armed guards was holding a black horse and presented it to Cervantes. He hesitated, but as soon as he accepted the mount, the line of guards opened up to let him through and gazed at him silently as he climbed onto the horse with Francesca in his arms. He was already trotting northwards when flames began to pour from the dome of Giordano's palace and Rome's sky became alive with scarlet and ashes. The couple rode by day, spending their nights in hostels and inns where the coins Cervantes had found in the horse's saddlebags allowed them to shelter from the cold and from suspicions.

Two whole days went by before Cervantes noticed the smell of almond essence on Francesca's lips and saw the dark circles that were beginning to show round her eyes. Every night, when the girl offered him her naked body with abandon, Cervantes knew she was wasting away in his hands, that the poisoned goblet with which Giordano had wanted to free her and free himself of the curse was now burning in her veins and consuming her. During their journey they stopped at the best inns, where doctors and wise men examined her but were unable to determine what her ailment was. Francesca faded during the day, when she was barely able to speak or keep her eyes open, and came alive at night, in the darkness of the bed, bewitching the poet's senses and guiding his hands. One evening, at the end of the second week of their travels, he found her walking in the rain by a lake, near the hostel where they had stopped for the night. The rain ran down her body and the girl stood, open-armed, her face raised to heaven, as if she was hoping that the pearly drops covering her skin could tear out her accursed soul.

'You must leave me here,' she said. 'Forget me and continue on your journey.'

But Cervantes, who saw how the young woman's light was becoming fainter day by day, promised himself that he would never say farewell to her, that while there was a single breath left in her body he would fight to keep her alive. To keep her his.

They crossed the Pyrenees into the Peninsula through a pass near the Mediterranean coast and were soon on their way to the city of Barcelona. By then Cervantes had already completed a hundred pages of a manuscript he wrote every night while he watched Francesca trapped in the nightmares of her sleep. He felt that his words, the images and the perfumes conjured up by his writing were now the only means of keeping her alive. Every night, when she fell into his arms and succumbed to sleep, Cervantes tried feverishly to rewrite her soul through a thousand and one fictions. When, a few days later, his mount dropped dead near the walls of Barcelona, the play he had written was already finished and Francesca seemed to have recovered her colour and the sparkle of her eyes. While he rode, he had been daydreaming that he would find shelter and hope in that city by the sea, that a friendly soul would lead him to someone who would print his manuscript, and that once people read his story and became immersed in the universe of images and poetry he had created, the Francesca he had fashioned with paper and ink and the one who lay dying in his arms every night would become as one and she would return to a world where malediction and hardship could be defeated by the power of words, a world in which God, wherever he was hiding, would allow him to live with her one more day.

(Extract from *The Secret Chronicles of the City of the Damned*, by Ignatius B. Samson. Published by Barrido y Escobillas, S.A., Barcelona 1924)

BARCELONA, 1569

They buried Francesca di Parma two days later beneath a flaming sky that glided over the calm sea and lit up the sails of the boats anchored at the port. The young girl had expired during the night in Cervantes's arms, in the room they occupied on the top floor of an old building on Calle Ancha. The printer Antoni de Sempere and Sancho were both with him when she opened her eyes for the last time and, smiling at Cervantes, murmured 'Free me.'

That afternoon Sempere had finished printing an edition of the second version of *A Poet in Hell*, a play in three acts by Don Miguel de Cervantes Saavedra, and had brought with him a copy to show the author, who was too downcast to even read his name on the cover. The printer, whose family owned a small plot of land near the old gate of Santa Madrona, next to Calle de Trenta Claus, offered to have the young woman buried in that humble graveyard, where, in the worst times of the Inquisition, the Sempere family had saved books from being burned by hiding them in coffins and interring them in what was a burial ground-cum-book sanctuary. Overcome with gratitude, Cervantes accepted.

The following day, after setting fire, for the second and last time, to his *Poet in Hell* on the sands of the strand – where one day Bachelor Sansón Carrasco was to defeat the ingenious knight Alonso Quijano – Cervantes abandoned the city and departed, this time holding the memory and the light of Francesca in his soul.

BARCELONA, 1610

Four decades were to pass before Miguel de Cervantes returned once more to the city where he had buried his innocence. A sea of misfortunes, failures and sorrows had dogged the story of his days. The sweetness of recognition, even in its most wretched and miserly form, had not smiled upon him until his later years. And while his admired contemporary, the playwright and adventurer Lope de Vega, had reaped fame, fortune and glory since his youth, Cervantes was awarded no laurels until it was too late, because applause can only be valued when it comes at the right moment. When it is a faded, withered flower it is no more than an insult and an offence.

By the year 1610, Cervantes was at last able to consider himself a famous author, even if one of very modest fortune, because money, the filthy lucre, had avoided him all his life and did not seem ready to change its mind in the final stages of his existence. Leaving aside the ironies of fate, experts on Cervantes maintain that he was happy during those three short months he spent in Barcelona in the year 1610, even if there are others who doubt whether he ever set foot in the city. Others still would protest vehemently at the mere suggestion that any of the events referred to in this modest apocryphal romance could have happened at any moment or place save in the decadent imagination of some heartless scribe.

Yet if we are to believe the legend and accept the currency

of fantasy and dreams, we can be sure that in those days Cervantes dwelt in a small studio opposite the harbour wall, with large windows open to the Mediterranean light that were not distant from the room where Francesca di Parma had died in his arms, and that every day he sat there to write some of the works that were to bring him so much fame, especially beyond the frontiers of his native kingdom. The building where he lived belonged to his old friend Sancho, who was now a wealthy merchant and father of six, with an affable nature that even his dealings with the world's ignominy had not managed to eradicate.

'And what are you writing, Master?' Sancho would ask every day when he saw him step out into the street. 'My esteemed wife is still awaiting further feats of valour and lance from our beloved Knight of La Mancha . . .'

Cervantes would just smile and never replied to his question. Sometimes, when it was getting dark, he would walk over to the printing press still run by old Antoni de Sempere and his son on Calle de Santa Ana, next to the church. Cervantes liked to spend time among books and pages waiting to be assembled, chatting with his old friend the printer and avoiding all mention of the memory they both kept alive in their minds.

One night, when it was time to leave the workshop until the following day, Sempere sent his son home and closed the shop doors. The printer seemed uneasy and Cervantes knew something had been bothering his good friend for the past few days.

'The other day a gentleman came by asking after you,' Sempere began. 'White hair, very tall, and his eyes were . . .'

'Like the eyes of a wolf,' Cervantes completed.

Sempere nodded.

'Precisely. He told me he was an old friend of yours and would like to see you if you ever happened to be in town . . . I wouldn't be able to tell you why, but the moment he left, I was seized by a great anxiety and began to think he must be the person you told me and good old Sancho about one fateful night in a tavern next to the basilica of Santa María del Mar. Needless to say, he wore a small silver angel on his lapel.'

'I thought you'd forgotten that story, Sempere.'

'I don't forget what I print.'

'I hope you didn't think of keeping a copy?'

Sempere gave him a tepid smile. Cervantes sighed.

'What did Corelli offer for your copy?'

'Enough for me to retire and hand over my business to the sons of Sebastián de Cormellas – and thus perform a good deed.'

'And did you sell it to him?'

Sempere did not reply. Instead, he turned round, walked over to a corner of his workshop, knelt down and, lifting a couple of floorboards, recovered an object wrapped in pieces of cloth, which he left on the table in front of Cervantes.

The novelist stared at the package for a few seconds and, at a nod from Sempere, removed the cloths to reveal the only extant copy of *A Poet in Hell*.

'May I take it with me?'

'It's yours,' answered Sempere. 'By virtue of authorship, and by payment of its publication costs.'

Cervantes opened the book and scanned the first few lines.

'A poet is the only being whose eyesight improves with age,' he said.

'Are you going to meet him?'

Cervantes smiled.

'Do I have a choice?'

A couple of days later, Cervantes went out for his customary long walk in the city, despite Sancho's warning that, according to the fishermen, a storm was brewing over the sea. At noon it began to rain heavily and black clouds covered the sky, throbbing with flashes of lightning and loud thunderclaps that seemed to be hammering the walls and threatening to destroy the entire city. Cervantes stepped into the cathedral to shelter from the storm. The church was deserted and the novelist sat in one of the pews of a side chapel where hundreds of candles burned warmly in the gloom. He was not surprised when he saw Andreas Corelli sitting next to him, his eyes fixed on the Christ figure hanging above the altar.

'Your Grace doesn't look a day older,' said Cervantes.

'Nor has your wit lessened, dear friend.'

'But perhaps my memory has, because I think I've forgotten that you and I were ever friends . . .'

Corelli shrugged.

'There he is, crucified to purge the sins of men, with no resentment, and you can't even forgive this poor devil . . .' Cervantes looked at him severely. 'Don't tell me blasphemy offends you now,' added Corelli.

'Blasphemy only offends whoever utters it to mock others.'

'It's not my intention to mock you, dear Cervantes.'

'What is your intention then, *Signore* Corelli?'

'To beg forgiveness of you?'

A long silence ensued between the two.

'One does not beg forgiveness with words.'

'I know. And what I'm offering is not words.'

'I hope it won't bother you if my enthusiasm flags when I hear the term "offer" from your lips.'

'Why should it bother me?'

'Perhaps Your Excellency has gone mad from reading too many missals? Perhaps you have started to believe, *Signore*, that you're riding through this vale of darkness to right the wrongs that our Saviour left for us all when he abandoned ship.'

Corelli crossed himself and smiled, baring those sharp, wolfish teeth.

'Amen,' he pronounced.

Cervantes stood up, bowed and turned to leave.

'Your company is most agreeable, dear *arcangelo*, but in the present circumstances I prefer the company of thunder and lightning. I'm off to enjoy the storm in peace.'

Corelli sighed.

'First listen to my offer.'

Cervantes walked slowly towards the exit. The cathedral door was slowly closing in front of him.

'I've seen this trick before.'

Corelli was waiting for him deep in the shadows of the doorway. Only his eyes were visible, lit up by the reflection of the candles.

'You once lost what you loved most, or what you thought you loved most, in exchange for the possibility of creating a masterpiece.'

'I never had a choice. You lied.'

'The choice was always in your hands, dear friend. And you know that.'

'Open the door.'

'The door is open. You can leave whenever you wish to.'

Cervantes stretched a hand out to the door and pushed it. The wind and the rain spat on his face. He stopped for a second before going out and, in the dark, the voice of Corelli whispered in his ear.

'I've missed you, Cervantes. My offer is simple: pick up the pen you've abandoned and reopen the pages you should never have closed. Bring your immortal book back to life and finish off the adventures of Don Quixote and his faithful squire for the pleasure and comfort of this poor reader whom you've turned into an orphan of wit and invention.'

'The story is finished, the Knight is buried and my voice is exhausted.'

'Do it for me and I'll give you back the company of what you loved most.'

From the door of the cathedral, Cervantes gazed at the ghostly tempest riding over the city.

'Do you promise?'

'I swear. In the presence of my Father and Lord.'

'Where's the catch this time?'

'There are no catches this time. This time, in exchange for the beauty of your creation, I'll give you what you most long for.'

And without further ado, the old novelist set off beneath the storm on the road to his destiny.

BARCELONA, 1616

That last night beneath the stars of Barcelona, old Sempere and Andreas Corelli accompanied the funeral cortege through the narrow streets of the city towards the private graveyard of the Sempere family, where many years earlier three friends with an unmentionable secret had buried the mortal remains of Francesca di Parma. The hearse advanced silently, lit up by torches, and people stood to one side. It made its way through the maze of passages and squares leading to the small cemetery that was secured with a gate of pointed spears. The hearse stopped when it reached the entrance. The two horsemen escorting the funeral carriage dismounted and, with the help of the coachman, unloaded the coffin, which bore no inscription or sign of any sort. Sempere opened the cemetery gates and let them through. They carried the coffin to the open grave that waited under the moon and let it rest on the ground. At a sign from Corelli, the attendants moved back to the entrance of the graveyard, leaving Sempere alone with the publisher. There was a sound of footsteps by the gate and when Sempere turned round he recognised old Sancho, who had come to bid farewell to his friend. Corelli gave a nod and the men let him through. When the three were standing before the coffin, Sancho knelt down and kissed the lid.

'I'd like to say a few words,' he whispered.

'Do proceed,' Corelli encouraged him.

'May God hold a great man and the best of friends in his everlasting glory. And if, in view of the present company, the Good Lord should assign duties to orders of a questionable rank, let the honour and the respect of his friends escort him on this his last journey to paradise, and may his immortal soul not lose its bearings along roads of sulphur and flames through some trickery of the defeated angel, for if that be so, by Heaven, I will gird myself with armour and lance and go forth to rescue him no matter how many plots and deceits the guardian of the underworld, in his malice, may decide to set before me.'

Corelli was looking at him coldly. Although he was scared to death, Sancho held his gaze.

'Is that all?' asked Corelli.

Sancho nodded, clasping his hands to stop them from shaking. Sempere looked questioningly at Corelli. The publisher took a few steps towards the coffin and, to everyone's surprise and alarm, opened it.

Cervantes's corpse lay inside the coffin clad in a Franciscan habit. His face was uncovered, his eyes were open and he had one hand on his chest. Corelli lifted Cervantes's hand and placed the book he carried with him underneath it.

'My friend, I hereby give these pages back to you: the sublime third and final part of the greatest of fables that you were good enough to write for this humble reader who knows that men will never be worthy of such beauty. That is why we bury it with you, so that you can take it to meet the person who has been waiting for you all these years and to whom, knowingly or not, you have always wished to return. Thus your greatest wish has been granted, your destiny and final prize.'

After those words, Corelli sealed the coffin.

'Here lie Francesca di Parma, a pure soul, and Miguel de Cervantes, light among poets, pauper among men and Prince of Parnassus. They will rest in peace among books and words and their eternal repose will never be perturbed or known by other mortals. May this place become a secret, a mystery whose origin and end will remain unknown. And may the spirit of the greatest teller of tales ever to walk the earth inhabit it forever more.'

Years later, on his deathbed, old Sempere would explain how at that very instant he thought he saw Andreas Corelli shed a tear which, when it hit Cervantes's tomb, turned to stone. He knew then that on that rock he would embark upon building a sanctuary, a cemetery of ideas and inventions, of words and marvels, a sanctuary that would grow over the ashes of the Prince of Parnassus and would, one day, house the greatest of all libraries, the one in which every persecuted title, every book hated through men's ignorance and spite would seek shelter, and wait there until it once again found the reader that every book carries within it.

'Cervantes, my friend,' he said, as he took his leave. 'Welcome to the Cemetery of Forgotten Books.'

*

This story is a simple divertimento that plays with some of the less known and less documented elements of the great author's life, in particular his journey to Italy in his youth and his stay or stays in Barcelona, the only city he mentions repeatedly in his work.

Unlike his admired contemporary Lope de Vega, who enjoyed great success from the start, Cervantes's pen was a late one and one that received little reward and recognition. The last years of the life of Miguel de Cervantes Saavedra were the most fertile of his turbulent literary career. After the publication of the first part of Don Quixote *in 1605, perhaps the most famous work in the history of literature and the precursor of the modern novel, a period of relative calm and recognition allowed him to publish in 1613 the* Exemplary Novels *and the following year his* Journey to Parnassus.

In 1615 the second part of Don Quixote *appeared. Miguel de Cervantes would die the following year in Madrid and would be buried, or so it was believed for years, in the convent of the Barefoot Trinitarians.*

There is nothing to prove that Cervantes ever wrote a third part of his most brilliant creation.

As of today, it is still not known for certain where his remains are buried.

A CHRISTMAS TALE

Translated by Lucia Graves

There was a time when the streets of Barcelona were tinted with gaslight at night, and at dawn the city awoke surrounded by a forest of chimney stacks that poisoned the sky with crimson. In those days Barcelona resembled a precipitous pile of basilicas and palaces, all tangled into a labyrinth of narrow streets and tunnels and trapped beneath a permanent mist, from which an imposing tower protruded. The building was shaped like a cathedral tower, with a Gothic spire, gargoyles and rose windows, and on its top floor lived the richest man in town, a lawyer named Eveli Escrutx.

Every night his silhouette could be seen outlined behind the golden glow of the attic window, watching the city at his feet like a sombre sentry. Escrutx had already made a fortune in his early youth by defending the interests of kid-gloved murderers, financiers who had grown rich in Latin America and industrialists of the new generation of steam and textile mills. They said that the hundred most powerful families in Barcelona paid him an exorbitant annuity in exchange for his counsel, and that all manner of statesmen and petty generals with imperial pretensions would queue up to be received in his office at the top of the tower. They said he never slept, that he spent the nights gazing at Barcelona from his large window and that he hadn't left the tower since the death of his wife thirty-three years earlier. They said the loss had driven a knife through his soul, that he hated everything and everyone, and that the only thing that drove him was his desire to watch the world consume itself with its own greed and meanness.

Escrutx had no friends or confidants. He lived alone at the top of the tower save for the company of Candela, a blind servant who, it was rumoured, was a bit of a witch and wandered through the streets of the old town offering sweets to poor children who were never seen again. The lawyer's only known passion, apart from the maid with her secret arts, was chess. Every year, on Christmas Eve, Escrutx would invite a person from Barcelona to meet him in his attic. He would serve him a delicious meal, washed down with the most superb wines. Then, at the stroke of midnight, when the bells rang from the cathedral, Escrutx would pour out two glasses of absinthe and challenge his guest to a game of chess. The lawyer promised the contender that if he won, he would hand over to him his entire fortune and properties. But if he lost, the guest would have to sign a contract whereby the lawyer became the exclusive owner and executor of his immortal soul. Every Christmas Eve.

Candela would ride through the streets of Barcelona in the lawyer's black carriage in search of a player. Beggars or bankers, murderers or poets, it made no difference. The game went on until dawn on Christmas Day. When the blood-red sun rose over the snow-capped rooftops of the Gothic quarter, the opponent invariably realised that he had lost the challenge. He walked out into the cold streets, carrying with him only the clothes on his back, while the lawyer picked up an emerald-coloured glass bottle, wrote the name of the loser on it, and added it to a display cabinet that held dozens of identical bottles.

They say that on that particular Christmas, the last in his long life, Escrutx, the lawyer, sent his white-eyed and black-lipped Candela, once again, to scour the streets in search of a new victim. A snowstorm loomed over the city, its cornices and terraced roofs all nickel-plated with ice. Flocks of bats fluttered between the cathedral towers and a red-hot copper moon poured its light over the narrow streets. The black steeds pulling the carriage stopped suddenly at the entrance to Calle del Obispo, their frosty breath betraying their fear. The silhouette stepped out of the fog, holding a bunch of red roses and wearing a long bride's veil that merged into the whiteness of the snow. Candela felt intoxicated by the woman's perfume and invited her to step into the carriage. She tried to feel her face, but all she found was ice and lips that were moist with bile. She took her to the tower, which in those days stood over the ruins of an old graveyard next to Calle Aviñón.

They say that when Escrutx saw her, he was struck dumb and ordered Candela to leave the room. The guest for that last Christmas Eve removed her veil and the lawyer, a soul wearied with age and eyes blinded by bitterness, thought he recognised the face of his deceased wife. Her lips were red and she shone like porcelain, and when Escrutx asked her her name she only smiled. Soon the midnight bells rang and the chess game began. Later, they would say that the lawyer was already tired, that he allowed himself to be defeated and that it was Candela who, driven mad with jealousy, started the blaze that would consume the tower, provoking an early dawn over the dark-purple skies of Barcelona. A group of children who had gathered round a bonfire in Plaza de San Jaime swore that a few moments before the flames streamed out of the windows they saw the lawyer step onto the balustrade, which was crowned with angels of alabaster, and open the emerald-green bottles to the wind, releasing plumes of vapour that dispersed into tears over all the terraced roofs of Barcelona. Serpents of fire knotted round one another as they ascended to the very top of the tower and the lawyer's silhouette was seen for the last time clasping his bride of fire, leaping from the tower into the void, their bodies crumbling into ashes which the wind took with it before they struck the cobblestones. The tower fell at daybreak, like a skeleton of shadows folding upon itself.

The legend ends by stating that after the collapse of the tower, a conspiracy of silence and forgetfulness perpetually deleted the name of the lawyer Escrutx from the city's chronicles. Poets and people with a pure spirit swear that even today, if one looks up to the heavens on Christmas Eve, one can still make out the ghostly shape of the burning tower in the midnight sky and see Escrutx, blinded by tears and repentance, freeing the first of the emerald-green bottles in his collection, the one that bore his name. But others will affirm that on that accursed dawn there were many who turned up at the ruins of the tower to take away one of the smouldering fragments, and that the charred remains of Candela's carriage can still be heard among the shadows of the old town, always in the dark, in search of the next candidate.

ALICIA, AT DAWN

Translated by Lucia Graves

The house where I last saw her no longer exists. In its place stands one of those buildings that slips from one's view and stamps its shadow on the sky. And yet, even today, every time I pass by, I remember those accursed days of Christmas 1938 when Calle Muntaner's long slope was lined with trams and palatial mansions. I was barely thirteen at the time, earning a few céntimos a week as an errand boy for a pawnshop on Calle Elisabets. The owner, Don Odón Llofriu, one hundred and fifteen kilos of meanness and suspicion, presided over his bazaar of trinkets complaining even of the air breathed by that shit of an orphan – one of the thousands the war spat out – whom he never called by his name.

'For heaven's sake, kid, turn off that light bulb, these are no times for luxuries! Mop the floor by candlelight, it stimulates the retina.'

And so our days went by, amid turbulent news from the National Front, which was advancing towards Barcelona, rumours of shootings and murders in the streets of the red-light district, and sirens warning of air raids. It was on one of those days in December 1938, when snow and ash peppered the streets, that I saw her.

She was dressed in white and seemed to have materialised out of the mist that swept the streets. When she stepped into the shop she paused in the small rectangle of light sliced out from the darkness by the shop window. In her hands she held a black velvet folder which she proceeded to open on the counter without saying a word. A garland of pearls and sapphires shone in the gloom. Don Odón grabbed his magnifying glass and examined the piece. I followed the scene from the chink in the back-room door.

'The piece isn't bad, but these are no times for luxuries, miss. I'll give you fifty duros, and I'll still lose money, but it's Christmas Eve and one isn't made of stone.'

The girl folded the cloth again and headed for the door without batting an eyelid.

'Kid!' bellowed Don Odón. 'Follow her.'

'That necklace is worth at least a thousand duros,' I remarked.

'Two thousand,' Don Odón corrected. 'So we're not going to let her get away. Follow her to her home and make sure nobody clobbers her and cleans her out. She'll be back, like all of them.'

The girl's footprints were already vanishing under the white blanket when I went out into the street. I followed her through the labyrinth of alleyways and buildings gutted by bombs and poverty, until she emerged into Plaza del Peso de la Paja and I managed to catch sight of her getting into a tram that was just heading up Calle Muntaner. I ran after the tram and jumped onto the back step.

We travelled uphill, cutting black tracks in the canvas of snow spread by the blizzard, while evening began to fall and the sky turned the colour of blood. By the time we reached the crossing with Travesera de Gracia my bones were aching with cold. I was about to abandon my mission and make up some lie to satisfy Don Odón, when I saw her alight and walk towards the large entrance of the mansion. I jumped off the tram and ran to hide behind the corner of the property. The girl slipped through the garden gate. I peeped between the bars and saw her cross the line of trees surrounding the house. She stopped by the front steps and turned round. I wanted to run off, but the icy wind had already robbed me of any will. The girl studied me with a slight smile and stretched out a hand. I realised she'd mistaken me for a beggar.

'Come,' she said.

Night was falling when I followed her through the dark mansion. A faint halo blurred the outlines. Fallen books and frayed curtains punctuated a scene of broken furniture, slashed paintings and dark stains spattering the walls like bullet marks. We came to a large hall that housed a mausoleum of old photographs, all of them redolent of absence. The girl knelt down in a corner near a fireplace and lit a fire with sheets of newspaper and the remains of a chair. I moved a bit closer to the heat and accepted the mug of warm wine she was offering me. She knelt down beside me, her gaze lost in the flames. She told me her name was Alicia. Her skin was the skin of a seventeen-year-old, but she was betrayed by that serious, unfathomable look of those who have become ageless, and when I asked whether those photographs were of her family she didn't reply.

I wondered how long she'd been living there, alone, hiding in that mansion in her white dress that was coming apart at the seams, selling jewels off cheaply in order to survive. She'd left the black velvet folder on the mantelpiece. Every time she bent forward to poke the fire I couldn't help glancing at it and imagining the necklace inside. Hours later we heard the bells strike midnight as we lay cuddled up quietly in front of the fire, and I thought that was how my mother would have hugged me if I could remember her. When the flames began to die away I wanted to throw a book into the fire, but Alicia snatched it from me and started to read aloud from its pages until we fell asleep.

I left shortly before dawn, unlocking myself from her

embrace and running in the dark towards the gate with the necklace in my hands and my heart pounding with anger. I spent the first few hours of that Christmas Day with two thousand duros' worth of pearls and sapphires in my pocket, cursing those streets that were swamped with snow and fury, cursing those who had abandoned me among flames, until a weak sun plunged a spear of light through the clouds and I retraced my steps to the mansion, dragging that necklace that weighed like a tombstone and was stifling me, hoping only to find her still asleep, asleep forever, so I could leave the necklace back on the mantelpiece above the embers and then flee without ever having to remember her look and her warm voice, the only pure touch I had ever known.

The door was open and a pearly light dripped through the cracks in the ceiling. I found her lying on the floor, still holding the book in her hands, her lips poisoned with frost and her eyes open in her white, icy face. A red tear lingered on her cheek and the wind blowing through that large wide-open window was burying her under dusty snow. I left the necklace on her chest and fled back to the street, to mingle with the walls of the city and hide in its silences, avoiding my reflection in shop windows for fear of seeing a stranger.

Shortly afterwards the sirens sounded again, silencing the Christmas bells, and a swarm of black angels spread over the red sky of Barcelona, dropping columns of bombs that would never be seen as they hit the ground.

MEN IN GREY

Translated by Lucia Graves

He never told me his name and I'd never wanted to ask. He was waiting for me, as usual, on that old bench in the Retiro Park, wedged inside a long line of linden trees that were bare from the winter and the rain. Dark glasses obscured the depth of his eyes. He was smiling. I took a seat next to him at the other end of the bench. The messenger handed me the envelope and I put it away without opening it.

'Aren't you going to count it?'

I shook my head.

'You should. This time the fee has tripled. Plus expenses and travel.'

'Where to?'

'Barcelona.'

'I don't handle Barcelona. They know that. Give it to Sanabria.'

'We already did. There was a problem.'

I pulled out the envelope with the money and passed it back to him.

'I don't handle Barcelona. They know that very well.'

'Aren't you going to ask me who the customer is?'

His smile oozed venom.

'It's all in the envelope. The ticket for tonight's train is in your name at the Atocha left-luggage office. The minister has asked me to convey his most sincere personal gratitude. He never forgets a favour.'

The messenger with dark glasses stood up and, with a slight bow, prepared to set off in the rain. We'd been meeting for three years in that same corner of the park, always at dawn, and we'd never exchanged a single word beyond what was strictly necessary. I watched him slip on his black leather gloves. His hands opened like spiders. He noticed me watching him and paused.

'Is there a problem?'

'Simple curiosity. What do you tell your friends when they ask you what your job is?'

When he smiled, his cadaverous face seemed to fuse into the shroud of his raincoat.

'Cleaning. I tell them I work in cleaning services.'

I nodded.

'And you?' he asked. 'What do you tell them?'

'I don't have friends.'

Splinters of frozen mist slithered over the vaulted ceiling of Atocha Station when I proceeded along the deserted platform on that 9 January 1942 to catch the midnight express to Barcelona. The minister's gratitude had earned me a first-class ticket and the velvet sanctuary of a private compartment. Even in those dark days the last thing lost among professionals was courtesy. The train slid off, scraping trails of vapour in the shadows, and soon the city disappeared into a cloud of faint lights and barren land. Only then did I open the envelope and pull out the neatly folded sheets, typed at one and a half spaces in blue ink. I was surprised to discover that there was no photograph in the envelope and wondered whether the only picture of the customer had been handed to Sanabria. I only had to read a couple of lines of the report to realise that this time there would be no photograph.

I switched off the light in the compartment and abandoned myself to a sleepless night, until dawn stained the horizon with scarlet blood and the silhouette of Montjuïc stood out in the distance. Three years earlier I had promised myself that I would never return to Barcelona. I'd fled from my city with a poisoned soul. A forest of ghostly factories and a sulphurous haze enveloped us and, moments later, the city sucked us into a tunnel that smelled of soot and doom. I opened the briefcase and began to load my revolver magazine with the bullets Sanabria had taught me to use during the years when I was his apprentice in the streets of the red-light district. Nine-millimetre shells, with hollow points made to turn into red-hot metal jaws on impact and drill exit wounds the size of a fist. When I got off the train and faced the iron cathedral of the Estación de Francia, I was welcomed by an icy, damp wind. I'd forgotten that the city still reeked of gunpowder. I set off towards Vía Layetana under a curtain of powdery snow that floated in the watery shadows of dawn. The trams opened pathways through the layer of white, and people, grey and faceless, wandered under the breath of flickering lamps that cast a violet light on the streets. I crossed Plaza Palacio and entered the web of narrow side streets surrounding the basilica of Santa María del Mar. The ruins from the air raids remained largely intact. Guts of buildings disembowelled by bombs – deserted dining rooms, bedrooms and bathrooms – stood next to empty lots piled high with rubble that served as shelters for black marketeers selling coal and other ragged faces whose gaze remained fixed to the ground.

When I reached Calle Platería I stopped to stare at the skeleton of the building where I grew up. All that remained was part of the facade, damaged by fire, and the adjacent walls. One could still see the scars from the incendiary bombs that had drilled through the floors and spread a tornado of flames through the stairwell and the skylight. I walked over to the front door and remembered the name of the first girl I kissed there one summer's night in 1913. Her name was Merche and she lived on the third floor, in flat number one, with her blind mother who always disliked me. Merche never married. Later, I was told that in one of the explosions they'd seen her being tossed into the air from the balcony, naked and wrapped in flames, her body skewered onto a thousand hot glass splinters. The sound of a footstep behind me brought me back to the present. I turned to discover an ashen figure looking like a replica of the messenger with dark glasses. I could barely tell the difference between them any more. Their look and their breath always smelled of death.

'You, identity card,' he muttered triumphantly.

Here and there I noticed brief looks from passers-by and the hasty steps of emaciated figures. I examined the secret police agent. I reckoned he was just over forty, and weighed about seventy kilos. His shoulders were slightly bent and a few centimetres of his neck showed under the black scarf. A quick slash, with a short blade, could slice his throat and his jugular in less than a second: he would collapse to the ground, voiceless, shedding his life through his fingers over the canvas of dirty snow on which he stood. Men like that one had a family, and I had things to do. I offered him a tepid smile and the document stamped by the ministry. His arrogance vanished instantly and he gave it back to me with trembling hands.

'Please forgive me, sir. I didn't know . . .'

'Clear off.'

The agent nodded repeatedly and vanished behind the first corner he found. The bells of Santa María tolled behind me as I started walking again under the snow towards Calle Fernando to become another grey man merging with the flood of grey men that was beginning to clog up that winter morning. One of them, some twenty metres behind me, had been following me at a distance since the train station, probably convinced that I hadn't noticed his presence. I vanished into that comfortable, numb anonymity where murderers – professionals or mere amateurs – disguised themselves as accountants and trainees, and crossed the Ramblas towards Hotel Oriente. A doorman in uniform with a degree in reading people's eyes opened the door for me with a bow. The hotel retained its aura of a sunken ship. The receptionist recognised me instantly and brandished a hint of a smile. Through the half-open glass doors of the dining hall came the echo of an out-of-tune piano.

'Would the gentleman like room 406?'

'If it's available.'

I signed the hotel register while the receptionist signalled to a porter to take my briefcase and accompany me to the room.

'I know the way, thanks.'

A quick look from the receptionist and the porter beat a retreat.

'If there's anything we can do to make the gentleman's stay in Barcelona more pleasant, you only have to say.'

'Same as usual,' I replied.

'Yes, sir. Of course.'

I was on my way to the elevator when I stopped. The receptionist was still standing in his place, his smile frozen.

'Is Señor Sanabria staying in the hotel?'

He barely blinked, but it was enough for me.

'Señor Sanabria hasn't graced us with a visit for some time.'

Room 406 looked out over Paseo de la Rambla from a fourth floor with heavenly views over the spectre of a vanished city that was condemned to remember the pre-war years. My shadow waited for me below, crouching under the canopy of a newspaper stand. I closed the shutters, enough to fill the room with a pearly gloom, and lay down on my bed. The sounds of the city could be heard outside, creeping along the walls. I pulled the revolver out of the briefcase and, with my finger on the trigger, folded my hands over my chest and closed my eyes. I fell into a muddy, hostile sleep. Hours or minutes later I was awoken by moist lips brushing my eyelids. Candela's warm body was stretched out on the bed, her fingers, imperceptible, unfastening her clothes, and her white-sugar skin lit up by the glow from the street lamps.

'Such a long time,' she murmured, snatching the revolver from my hands and leaving it on the bedside table. 'If you like, I can stay all night.'

'I've got to work.'

'But you'll also have a bit of time for your Candela.'

Three years' absence had not erased the memory of Candela's body from my hands. These new times and the reopening of first-class hotels suited her well. Her breasts smelled of expensive perfume and I noticed a new firmness in her pale thighs, covered in those silk stockings she ordered from Paris. Patient and expert, Candela let me do as I wished until I'd quenched my thirst for her skin and moved to one side. I heard her walk over to the bathroom and run a tap. I got up and took the envelope with the money from the briefcase. I tripled her usual fee and left the folded notes on the chest of drawers. Then I lay on the bed and watched Candela as she walked over to the windows and opened the shutters. The snow falling behind the windowpanes left spots of shadow on her naked skin.

'What are you doing?'

'I like looking at you.'

'Aren't you going to ask me where he is?'

'Would you tell me if I did?'

She turned and sat down on the edge of the bed.

'I don't know where he is. I haven't seen him. It's the truth.'

I just nodded. Candela looked away and eyed the money on the chest of drawers.

'You're doing well,' she said.

'I can't complain.'

I began to get dressed.

'Do you have to go?'

I didn't reply.

'There's more than enough here for the whole night. If you like, I'll wait for you.'

'I'll be a long time, Candela.'

'I'm not in a hurry.'

I met Roberto Sanabria one night in 1917. It was a steamy August and the city was consumed with anger. Like almost every night, gunshots were heard in the neighbourhood before daybreak. I'd gone down to Paseo del Borne to fetch water from the fountain, and when I heard the shots I ran to hide in a doorway on Calle Montcada. Sanabria was lying in a black pool that spread at my feet like a slimy blanket, by the entrance to that narrow gap between old buildings that some people still call Calle de las Moscas, the street of flies. He held a smoking gun in his hands. I walked up to him and he smiled at me, with blood oozing from his lips.

'Don't worry, mate, I've got more lives than a cat.'

I helped him up and, supporting his considerable weight, brought him to a doorway in Calle de Baños Viejos, where we were attended by a large, morose woman with scabby skin. Sanabria had received two gunshots in the abdomen and had lost so much blood his skin was the colour of wax, but he didn't stop smiling at me while some quack who stank of muscatel cleaned his wounds with vinegar and surgical spirit.

'I owe you one, son,' he said before passing out.

Sanabria would survive that night and many other dark hours

of gunpowder and metal. Those were the days when Barcelona newspapers were steeped in reports warning that people were being killed in the streets. Unions for hired gunmen were doing well. Life was still as worthless as ever, but death had never been so cheap. It was Sanabria who, when I reached adulthood, taught me the trade.

'Unless you want to die a day labourer, like your father.'

To kill was a necessity, but to murder was an art, he maintained. His preferred tools were the revolver and the knife with a short curved blade that bullfighters used to finish a *faena* in the bullring with a quick dry stab. Sanabria taught me that one must only shoot a man in the face or in the chest, preferably at less than two metres' distance. He was a professional with principles. He didn't take on women or the elderly. Like so many others, he'd learned to kill in the Moroccan war. When he returned to Barcelona he started his career as a gunman in the ranks of the FAI,[3] but soon discovered that organised syndicates paid better and that their work was not polluted with high-sounding rhetoric. He liked music-hall shows and whores, interests which he instilled in me with paternal strictness and a scholarly touch.

'Nothing is truer in life than a good comedy or a good whore. Never treat them with disrespect or feel superior to them.'

It was Sanabria who introduced me to a seventeen-year-old Candela who carried the world on her skin and was destined to work in the best hotels, and to service council officials.

'Never fall in love with something that is priceless,' Sanabria advised me.

Once I asked him how many men he'd killed.

---

3   Iberian Anarchist Federation.

'Two hundred and six,' he replied. 'But better times are coming.'

My mentor was referring to the war that could already be sniffed in the air like the stench of a flooded sewer. Shortly before the summer of 1936, Sanabria told me that times were about to change and we'd soon have to leave Barcelona, because the city was reeling, with a stake plunged in its heart.

'Death, which always follows gold, is moving to Madrid,' he pronounced. 'And we're going with it. It's only a matter of time.'

The real bonanza began at the end of the war. The corridors of power twisted into new spider's webs and, just as my teacher had predicted, a million dead had only begun to quench the thirst for hatred that rotted the streets. Old contacts in the Barcelona organisation opened up big opportunities for us.

'No more killing poor devils in public urinals for a few pesetas,' Sanabria announced. 'We're now going to start working on quality clients.'

Almost two years of glory followed. Hard-working minds endowed with prodigious memories drew up endless lists of people who didn't deserve to live, miserable creatures whose breath contaminated the incorruptible spirit of the new era. Dozens of tremulous souls hid in dismal apartments fearing the light of day, without realising that they were living dead. Sanabria taught me how not to listen to their pleadings, their tears and moans, how to blow open their heads with a point-blank shot between the eyes before they could ask why. Death waited for them in the subway stations, in dark streets and in *pensiones* with no running water or light. Professors or poets, soldiers or intellectuals, they all recognised us the moment we exchanged glances. Some died without fear, calmly, eyes clear and fixed on their murderer. I don't remember their names, or what they did in life to earn death by my hands, but I remember their looks. Soon I lost count, or wished I could. Sanabria, who was beginning to feel the weight of years and the scars from staying in the business, handed me the best jobs.

'My bones are starting to complain. From now on I'll only deal with unimportant customers. One has to know when to stop.'

I used to meet the messenger with the dark glasses on the same bench of the Retiro Park once a week. There would always be an envelope and a new client. The money piled up in the account of a bank on Calle O'Donnell. The only thing Sanabria had not taught me was what to do with those stiff, scented, glossy notes straight out of the mint.

'Will they ever end?' I once asked the messenger.

It was the only time he removed his glasses. His eyes were as grey as his soul, dead and empty.

'There's always someone who doesn't adapt to progress.'

It was still snowing when I stepped out into the Ramblas. It was just an icy dust that didn't settle when it touched the ground and swirled about in the breeze, turning to specks of light in one's breath. I set off towards Calle Nueva, now reduced to a tunnel of darkness flanked by the forgotten carcasses of dilapidated dance halls and ghostly music-hall theatres that only a few years earlier had transformed the street into an avenue of light and noise until dawn. The pavements smelled of urine and coal. I walked down Calle Lancaster until I reached number thirteen. A couple of old street lamps hanging from the facade barely managed to scrape the darkness, but were sufficient to let one glimpse the poster nailed above the charred wooden door sealing the entrance.

THE SHADOW THEATRE

*Returns to Barcelona after a triumphant world tour to
present its new and magnificent puppet and automatons
show, with the exclusive and enigmatic first appearance
of the Paris music-hall star Madame Isabelle and her
exciting 'Dance of the Midnight Angel'.
Shows every night at midnight.*

I knocked twice with my fist, waited, then knocked again. About a minute went by before I heard footsteps on the other side of the large door. The oak panel opened a few centimetres to reveal the face of a woman with silvery hair and pupils so dilated they seemed to flood her eyes. A golden, liquid light poured from within.

'Welcome to the Shadow Theatre,' she announced.

'I'm looking for Señor Sanabria,' I said. 'I think he's expecting me.'

'Your friend isn't here, but if you wish to come in, the show is about to start.'

I followed the lady along a narrow corridor until we reached a staircase leading down to the basement. A dozen empty tables filled the auditorium. The walls were lined with black velvet and the footlights drilled needles of brightness through the vaporous atmosphere. Only a couple of customers languished on the edge of the darkness surrounding the auditorium. A drinks bar decorated with smoked mirrors and a pit for the pianist buried in a coppery light completed the scene. The closed scarlet curtain was embroidered with the figure of a harlequin puppet. I sat down at one of the tables in the auditorium facing the stage. Sanabria adored puppet shows. He used to say that puppets, more than anything else, reminded him of ordinary people.

'More than whores do.'

The barman served me what I supposed was a glass of brandy and walked away silently. I lit a cigarette and waited for the lights to dim. Once there was total darkness, the folds in the scarlet curtain slowly drew open. The figure of an exterminating angel, hanging from silver strings, descended onto the stage, flapping its black wings through puffs of blue vapour.

When, on the train to Barcelona, I'd opened the envelope containing the cash and the information, and had started to read the typed pages, I knew that this time there would be no photograph of the customer. There was no need. The night Sanabria and I had left Barcelona, my teacher, his hands stopping the bleeding that spurted over my chest, had fixed his eyes on mine and smiled.

'I owed you one, and I'm paying you back. We're quits now. One day somebody will come for me. One doesn't make it in this line of business without ending up sitting in the customer's chair. That's how it is. But when my time comes, and it's not that far off, I'd like it to be you.'

The ministerial report, as usual, spoke between the lines. Sanabria had returned to Barcelona three months earlier. His break with the network came from further back, when he'd refused to carry out a number of contracts, alleging that he was a man of principles in an age where principles no longer existed. The first mistake made by the ministry was to try to eliminate him. The second, a dreadful mistake, was to do it badly. From the first hit man they sent after him all that came back, by registered post, was his right hand. A man like Sanabria can be murdered, but he must never be insulted. A few days after his arrival in Barcelona, the operatives in the ministerial network began to be eliminated, one after the other. Sanabria worked by night and had perfected his skill with the short blade. Within two weeks he'd decimated the basic structure of the secret police in the city of Barcelona. By three weeks he'd begun to score in the most exclusive – and visible – sectors of the regime. Before panic spread, Madrid decided to send one of its best people to negotiate with Sanabria. The man from the ministry now rested beneath a marble stone in the morgue of the Raval quarter, with a wide smile knifed on his throat, identical to the smile that had ended the life of Lieutenant General Manuel Jiménez Salgado, shining star of the military government and a firm candidate for a brilliant career inside the ministries of the capital. That's when I was called. The report described the situation as a 'deep crisis'. Sanabria, in ministerial parlance, had decided to go freelance and had submerged himself in the Barcelona underworld in order to carry out a sort of personal vendetta against well-known members of the regime's military judiciary. The plot, said the report, must be 'rooted out, whatever the cost'.

'I was expecting you earlier,' murmured my mentor's voice in the dark. Even at his age the old murderer knew how to creep in the shadows with the same feline skill as in his youth.

'You look well,' I said.

Sanabria shrugged and pointed to the stage, where a lacquered wooden coffin was opening up to reveal the star of the automatons' show, Madame Isabelle and her 'Dance of the Midnight Angel'. The movements performed by Isabelle, a life-size puppet with human expressions, were hypnotic. Held up by filaments of light, she danced on the stage, catching the pianist's notes in flight.

'I come to see her every night,' murmured Sanabria.

'They're not going to let this continue, Roberto. If it's not me, it will be someone else.'

'I know. I'm glad it's you.'

We watched the automaton's dance for a few seconds, sheltering in the strange beauty of its movements.

'Who's pulling the strings?' I asked.

Sanabria just smiled back.

We left the Shadow Theatre shortly before daybreak, setting off down the Ramblas to the docks, a cemetery of masts in the mist. Sanabria wanted to see the sea for the last time, even if it was only that black, smelly water licking the steps of the quay. When a blade of amber cut across the skyline, Sanabria at last consented and we set off towards the room he rented in a third-rate brothel in Portal de Santa Madrona. Sanabria never felt safer than among his prostitutes. It was just a dark, damp cubicle, with no windows, that seemed to sway under the naked light bulb. A bare mattress was propped against the wall and a couple of bottles and dirty glasses completed the furniture.

'One day they'll come after you too,' said Sanabria.

We gazed at each other in silence and, having nothing left to say, I hugged him. He had the smell of a tired old man.

'Say goodbye to Candela for me.'

I closed the door of his room and walked off down that narrow corridor, with walls that sweated mould and ruin. A few seconds later the sound of the gunshot roared through the passageway. I heard the corpse slump onto the floor and flew down the stairs. One of the old whores watched me from a half-open door on the next landing, her eyes wet with tears.

I wandered aimlessly for a couple of hours through the accursed streets of the city before going back to the hotel. When I crossed the entrance hall the receptionist barely looked up from the hotel register. I took the elevator up to the top floor and walked all the way down the deserted corridor to my door at the end. I wondered whether Candela would believe me if I told her I'd let Sanabria go, that at that very moment our old friend was sailing on board a cruiser towards a safe destination. Perhaps, as always, a lie was what would most resemble the truth. I opened the door without turning on the light. Candela still lay asleep on the sheets, with the first breath of dawn clinging to her naked body. I sat on the edge of the bed and slid my fingertips down her back. She felt as cold as frost. Only then did I notice that what I'd taken for the shadow of her body was in fact blood spreading like an open flower over the bed. I turned round slowly and made out, obscured by the shadows, the barrel of the revolver pointing at me. The messenger's dark lenses shone on his face, beaded with sweat. He smiled.

'The minister gratefully thanks you for your invaluable collaboration.'

'But he doesn't trust my silence.'

'These are difficult times. The fatherland demands great sacrifices, my friend.'

I covered Candela's body with the sheet soaked in her blood.

'You never told me your name,' I said, turning my back to him.

'Jorge,' replied the messenger.

I spun round, the dagger's short blade just a flash of light between my fingers. The slash opened his abdomen at the pit of the stomach. The first shot from his gun went through my left hand. The second struck the top of one of the bedposts and pulverised it into a cascade of smouldering fragments. By then, the blade of the knife Sanabria admired so much had opened the messenger's throat, and the man lay on the floor choking on his own blood while his gloved hands tried desperately to keep his head joined to his trunk. I pulled out the revolver and stuck it in his mouth.

'I don't have friends.'

I took the train back to Madrid that very evening. My hand was still bleeding; the pain, like a red-hot splinter nailed into my memory. Otherwise, anyone could have taken me for another grey man amid the armies of grey men hanging from invisible strings that hovered over the scenery of those stolen times. Locked away in my compartment, gun in hand, gazing out of the window, I stared at that endless black night that opened up like a chasm over the bloodstained earth of the entire country. Sanabria's anger would be my anger, and Candela's skin would be my light. The wound that was drilling through my hand would never stop bleeding. When at dawn the infinite plain of Madrid came into view I smiled to myself. In just a few minutes my footsteps would become inscrutable, lost in the labyrinth of the city. As usual, my mentor had shown me the way, even in his absence. I knew that in all likelihood the papers would not mention me, that history books would try to bury my name amid political statements and fabrications. Little did it matter. Every day there would be more of us men in grey. Soon we'd be sitting next to you, in a café or on a bus, reading a newspaper or a magazine. The long night of history had only just begun.

KISS

I never told anybody, but getting that apartment was nothing short of a miracle. All I knew about Laura was that she worked part-time at the offices of the landlord on the first floor, and that she kissed like a tango. I met her on a July night when the skies blanketing Barcelona sizzled with steam and desperation. I had been sleeping on a bench in a nearby square when I was awakened by the brush of her lips.

Do you need a place to stay?

She led me to the lobby. The building was one of those vertical mausoleums that haunt the old town, a labyrinth of gargoyles and patched-up masonry, at the top of which you could still make out 1866 somewhere beneath the layer of soot.

I followed her upstairs, almost feeling my way in the darkness. The building creaked under my feet like an old ship. Laura never asked for any references, personal or financial. Good thing, because in prison you don't get either. The attic was the size of my former cell, a spare room perched over the endless roofworld of the old city.

I'll take it.

Truth be told, three years in the slammer had obliterated my sense of smell and the issue of voices leaking through the walls wasn't exactly a novelty for me. One man's hell is another's paradise lost.

Laura would come to me every night. Her cold skin and her misty breath were the only things that didn't burn during that scorching summer. At dawn she would silently vanish downstairs, leaving me to doze off during the day.

The neighbours had that meek kindness conferred by years of misery and oblivion. I counted six families, all with children and old-timers reeking of dead flowers and damp soil. My favourite was Don Florián, who lived below me and painted dolls and tin toys for a living. I spent weeks without venturing out of the building. Spiders were building arabesques in my doorway. But Doña Luisa, on the third floor, always brought me something to eat. Don Florián lent me old magazines and challenged me to endless domino matches. The kids in the building invited me to play hide-and-seek.

It was a good life. For the first time ever I felt welcomed. Even appreciated.

By midnight Laura would bring me her nineteen years wrapped in white silk and give herself to me as if it were the last time. I'd make love to her until the break of dawn, savouring in her body everything life had denied me. Afterwards, I'd dream in black and white, like dogs and cursed people. But even the lowest of the low sometimes get a taste of happiness in this world. That summer was mine.

When the demolition people came by in late August I mistook them for cops. The chief engineer told me he had nothing personal against squatters, but unfortunately they had to dynamite the place and raze it to the ground no matter what.

There must be a mistake.

Most chapters in my life begin with that line.

I ran downstairs to the landlord's office on the first floor looking for Laura. All I found was a coat hanger and two inches of dust. I went to Don Florián's. Fifty eyeless dolls rotting in the shadows. I went through the entire building looking for just one neighbour, one voice. Silent corridors lay covered in debris.

This property has been closed down since 1938, young man, the chief engineer informed me. *The bomb damaged the structure beyond repair.*

I believe we had some words. The wrong kind. My kind. I believe I pushed him. Down the stairs. Hard. This time the judge had a field day with me. My old cellmates, it turned out, were still waiting.

After all, you always come back.

Hernán, the library guy, found a ten-year-old newspaper article about the bombardment during the civil war. In the photograph the bodies are lined up in pine boxes, disfigured by shrapnel, but they were still recognisable to me. A shroud of blood spreads over the cobblestones. Laura is dressed in white, her hands crossed over her open chest.

*

It's been almost two years now, but in prison you live or die by memories. The guards think they're smart, but she knows how to sneak in past any walls.

At midnight I am awakened by the brush of her icy lips. She brings greetings from Don Florián and the others.

You'll love me always, won't you? she asks.

And I say yes.

GAUDÍ IN MANHATTAN

Translated by Carlos Ruiz Zafón

Many years later, as I watched the funeral procession for my master parade down Paseo de Gracia, I remembered the year I met Gaudí and my fate was sealed. I had arrived in Barcelona that autumn intent on gaining admission to the School of Architecture. My dreams of conquering the city depended on a grant that barely covered my tuition and the rent on a small room in a boarding house on Calle del Carmen. Unlike most of my fellow students, graced with patrician airs and fashionable attire, my wardrobe consisted solely of an old black suit I had inherited from my father that was several sizes too big and a few inches too short. In March 1908, Don Jaume Moscardó, the head of the department, summoned me to his office to pass judgement on my sterling academic performance and, I suspected, my lacklustre appearance.

'You look like a beggar, Miranda,' he pronounced. 'How do you expect to get work designing beautiful buildings when you look like a car crash? If you're running short of funds maybe I could offer you a hand. Word among the faculty is that you're quite a sharp young man. Tell me, what do you know about Gaudí?'

*

Gaudí. The mere mention of his name gave me the shivers. I had grown up dreaming of his impossible vaults, his neo-

Gothic reefs of stone and his futuristic primitivism. Gaudí was the principal reason I had wanted to become an architect. My main goal in life, other than not perishing from hunger during that first year of study, had been to try to absorb a tiny portion of the prodigious science with which that great man, my modern Prometheus, plotted the shape of his creations.

'I'm his greatest admirer,' I managed to answer.

Moscardó chuckled.

'I feared as much.'

I could detect in his voice the vaguely condescending tone that most people adopted when speaking about Gaudí in those days. Death bells were tolling everywhere for what some of us still called modernism, or art nouveau, and the majority simply deemed it an affront to good taste. The self-appointed new guard imposed a doctrine based on bare essentials, according to which the delirious baroque facades that in time would become the city's pride and joy were sentenced to public crucifixion. Over the years, Gaudí had earned a reputation as an extravagant, celibate and reclusive lunatic. He was generally regarded as a misguided visionary who was indifferent to fame and fortune, and whose sole obsession was the construction of his phantasmagoric cathedral, the Sagrada Familia. He had been living alone in the crypt of the unfinished church for years, sleeping on a camp bed in a corner of the sculpture workshop. He spent most of his time dressed in rags, drawing plans that defied the laws of geometry. He was utterly convinced that the only client he was answerable to was the Almighty.

'Gaudí is insane,' continued Moscardó. 'Now he's trying to put a madonna the size of the Colossus of Rhodes on top of Casa Milà in the heart of the city. He has balls, I'll give him that. But, crazy or not, there's never been and never will be an architect remotely like him.'

'That is my opinion precisely, sir,' I ventured.

'So then you'll have realised it's useless trying to become his successor?'

The august professor must have read the disappointment in my eyes.

'But perhaps you could become his assistant. One of the Llimona brothers working with him mentioned the other day that Gaudí is looking for somebody who speaks English. God knows why. If you ask me, what he really needs is someone who speaks Spanish because the stubborn son-of-a-bitch refuses to speak anything but Catalan, especially when ministers, princes and various court eunuchs from Madrid show their faces. I volunteered to find him a suitable candidate.'

A spy, more like, I thought, smiling meekly and pretending to be unaware of his real motives.

'I see,' I muttered.

'*Doo yoooo espik eengleesh*, Miranda?'

I guessed that the sounds emerging from Moscardó's mouth were supposedly the language of Shakespeare, although with his accent they could just as easily have been Aramaic or the symptom of some insidious throat infection. I swallowed hard and summoned the spirit of Machiavelli, patron saint of the expedient manoeuvre.

'*A leet-l*,' I replied in equally undecipherable gibberish.

Moscardó beamed, relieved.

'Well, *congratoolayshons*, and may the Lord have mercy on you.'

*

Later that afternoon, as the sun was beginning to sink, I set out for the building site of the Sagrada Familia. In those days, the confines of the city began to fade around Paseo de San

Juan, beyond which unfolded a mirage of fields, factories and isolated buildings that stood like lonely sentinels in the grid of a future promised land. Soon I spied the spires of the new church outlined against the twilit skies. A night watchman was waiting for me at the entrance holding a gas lantern. I followed him through portals and arches until we reached the stairs leading down to Gaudí's workshop. As I entered the crypt I felt my heart begin to race. A menagerie of fabulous creatures swayed in the shadows and at the centre of the workshop four skeletons were suspended from the vault above in a macabre ballet. Below them I found a small white-haired man with the bluest eyes I'd ever encountered – somehow he had the air of a person who has seen things other mortals can only dream of. He dropped a notepad on which he had been sketching and smiled at me. It was the smile of a child, full of magic and mystery.

'Moscardó will have told you that I'm a raving madman who never speaks Spanish. The truth is, I do speak Spanish, but only when it pisses somebody off. What I don't speak is a word of English, and on Saturday I'm boarding a ship bound for New York. I understand that you speak it, young man? English, I mean.'

That night I felt like the luckiest man in the universe as I shared Gaudí's conversation and half of his dinner, just a handful of nuts and some lettuce leaves sprinkled with a hint of olive oil. When we had finished, Gaudí poured two glasses of water and looked at me with his penetrating stare.

'Do you know what a skyscraper is?'

For want of any personal experience in the matter, I dusted off various notions we had received in class about the Chicago School, steel-reinforced concrete and the invention of the moment, the Otis elevator.

'Nonsense,' Gaudí cut in. 'A skyscraper is simply a cathedral for people who, instead of believing in God, believe in money.'

It was thus that I learned Gaudí had received an offer from a fabulously wealthy tycoon to design and build a skyscraper in the heart of Manhattan, and that my role was to be his interpreter during a meeting that was to take place between the architect and his mysterious client nine days later, at the Waldorf-Astoria.

*

I spent the next three days secluded in my room perusing a pile of English grammar books and dictionaries that I had borrowed in haste from the college library. On Friday we took the train to Calais, whence we would cross the English Channel to Southampton to board the *Lusitania*. As soon as we boarded the ship, Gaudí retired to his cabin, overwhelmed by homesickness. He wouldn't emerge until the following day, when I found him at dusk, seated at the bow of the ship watching the sun bleed over a horizon of sapphire and copper.

'Now, *that* is real architecture,' he muttered. 'Mist and light. If you really want to learn, Miranda, you have to observe nature. All the answers lie within.'

For me, the crossing of the Atlantic became a blinding crash course in itself. Every afternoon we walked around the deck discussing blueprints, techniques and the secrets of the trade. Lacking better company, and perhaps aware of the almost religious devotion he inspired in me, Gaudí offered his friendship and showed me the sketches he had dreamed up for his skyscraper, a Wagnerian needle of stone and light that, in my humble opinion, could easily become the most prodigious structure ever created by man – were it ever built.

Gaudí's ideas were breathtaking, yet I could not help but

notice that there was no warmth or even a shadow of interest in his voice whenever he talked about the project. It seemed obvious to me that his heart was elsewhere. The night before our arrival I dared ask the question that had been gnawing at me since we set sail.

'Master,' I ventured hesitantly, 'why do you want to embark on an endeavour that could take you away from your home and your work at the Sagrada Familia for months, even years?'

Gaudí smiled, sadly.

'Sometimes, to do the Lord's work you have to shake the hand of the devil.'

He then told me that if he agreed to build this Babel in the heart of New York, his client would underwrite the completion of the Sagrada Familia. I still remember his words. *God is patient, but I won't live forever . . .*

*

We arrived in New York as the sun set. A storm was brewing and a malevolent mist slithered between the spires of Manhattan, the metropolis trapped beneath scarlet skies that pulsated with lightning and the smell of sulphur. A black carriage was waiting for us at the Chelsea pier and carried us through darkening canyons of stone towards the centre of the island. Spirals of steam rose from the cobblestones, and trams, carriages and pedestrians swarmed furiously across the infernal hive of a city built with layer upon layer of grandiose mansions. Gaudí beheld the spectacle with sombre eyes. The clouds were pierced by swords of blood-tinted light as we turned into Fifth Avenue and saw the silhouette of the grand Waldorf-Astoria looming ahead, a mausoleum of gables and towers erected on 34th Street at the site where, twenty years later, the Empire State Building would rise from the ashes of the grandest hotel the city had ever seen.

The manager of the Waldorf greeted us in person at the door, informing us that our client would see us later that evening. I was translating as he spoke, whispering to Gaudí, who simply nodded. We were escorted to a luxurious room on the sixth floor from which we could see the storm clouds massing over the city. Moments later, rain began to pelt the windows. I gave the bellboy a handsome tip and thereby learned that our client lived in a suite occupying the entire top floor and that, to the bellboy's knowledge, this person had never emerged from their quarters. When I asked what kind of person he was and what he looked like, the boy departed in a hurry, leaving us to witness the gathering storm in silence.

*

When the time for our appointment came, Gaudí stood up and gave me an anguished look. An elevator operator attired in red was waiting for us at the end of the corridor. As we ascended floor by floor in that steel cage, I noticed that Gaudí was growing increasingly pale and that he barely seemed capable of holding the portfolio containing his sketches, so I took it from him. The doors opened onto a spacious marble foyer leading to a long corridor that disappeared into shadows. As the elevator operator closed the doors behind us and the light from within faded away, I noticed the flame of a candle flickering in the hallway. It advanced towards us, held by a svelte figure dressed in white. Long, black hair framed the fairest face I had ever seen, with blue eyes that pierced the soul. Eyes that were identical to Gaudí's.

'Welcome to New York.'

Our client was a woman possessed of a disturbing beauty, almost painful to behold. A Victorian novelist would have described her as an angel, but I failed to perceive anything angelic about her presence. Her movements appeared feline, her smile vaguely reptilian. She took us to a dim drawing room in which the curtains seemed to catch fire with each burst of lighting. We sat down. One by one, Gaudí produced his sketches while I translated his words. An hour, or an eternity, later, the lady fixed her eyes on me and, licking her carmine lips, intimated that I should now leave her alone with Gaudí. I looked at the master, hesitant. He nodded slowly.

Against my better judgement, I obeyed and left the room, walking down the corridor towards the foyer, where the elevator doors were already beginning to open. Once inside, I looked back for a second. The woman was leaning over Gaudí and, taking his face in her hands with infinite tenderness, she kissed him on the lips. Just then a flare of lightning ignited the shadows and, for a split second, it seemed as if the person holding my master's face was no lady, but a dark, cadaverous figure with a great black dog seated at its feet. The last thing I saw before the elevator doors closed were the tears on Gaudí's cheeks.

*

When I got back to the room I lay on the bed, invaded by a growing sense of nausea. In a matter of minutes, I fell into a deep and blinding sleep. When the first light of dawn caressed my face, I woke up with a start and rushed to my master's chamber. The bed was still made and there was no sign of Gaudí. I went down to the reception desk to ask if anybody knew his whereabouts. One of the doormen told me he'd seen a man who looked like my master leaving the hotel a few minutes earlier.

'I asked him if he wanted a cab, but he didn't seem to notice me. He crossed Fifth Avenue without looking where he was going and a tram almost hit him. I called after him, but he just kept on walking . . .'

I could not explain exactly why, but I had a feeling I knew where I would find him.

'Is there a church around here?' I asked.

Following the doorman's instructions, I walked north to St Patrick's Cathedral. It was very early in the morning and the church was deserted. I stood on the threshold and caught sight of the master, kneeling in the aisle by the front pew. I walked down the aisle and took a seat at his side. He turned to look at me. His face seemed to have aged twenty years in one night, transformed by that absent air that would accompany him until the last of his days.

'You should watch out for the trams, Master.'

He nodded.

'That's what everybody keeps telling me.'

He made the sign of the cross, stood up and then sat down beside me, his eyes lost in the altar.

'Who was that woman, Master?'

He looked at me, bemused. I understood then that only I had seen the lady in white. I did not dare imagine what the master had seen, but I was positive about one thing: they both shared the same gaze.

That evening we took the boat back home. We stood at the stern of the ship and watched the lights of New York evaporate on the horizon. Then, once we had reached the open sea and were being lashed by a cold wind, Gaudí took the portfolio containing his sketches and threw it into the ocean.

'Master! Why?' I asked, horrified. 'What about the funds for the Sagrada Familia?'

Gaudí took a deep breath, his hand shaking as he gripped the rail and faced the cold wind blowing in from the North Atlantic.

'God is patient, and I cannot afford the price that is asked of me,' he whispered.

During the trip home, I would ask him many times about that price, and the identity of his client. Many times he would smile at me wearily and simply shake his head. Days later, en route to Barcelona, I had to face the fact that my services as an interpreter would no longer be needed. I spent the last few hours on the train from Paris brooding, fearful of my return to the routine of student life, away from the master. Gaudí seemed to sense my sadness and, before he bid me farewell at the station, he embraced me and told me I could visit him at his study anytime I wanted.

*

The day after our arrival I returned to the School of Architecture, where Moscardó was waiting to interrogate me.

'So?' he said.

'Nothing much,' I offered. 'We went to Manchester to visit a factory that makes steel rivets, but after three days Gaudí said he wanted to come back home because the British only serve boiled beef and hate the Virgin Mary.'

Moscardó stared without blinking. I shrugged.

'That's about it.'

He chuckled.

'Crazy as a cuckoo,' he muttered to himself, deeply disappointed.

*

Months later, during one of my many visits to the Sagrada Familia building site, I found myself staring at one of the new sculptures on the pediment. I would have recognised that face anywhere. The lady in white. Her figure, intertwined in a whirl of snakes, invoked an angel with pointed wings, luminous and cruel. I stayed there for a long time, until the sun faded and a shroud of darkness crept over the stone, and watched as her face sank into the shadows, smiling at me.

*

Gaudí and I never talked about what had happened in New York. Whenever I brought up the subject, he would smile and silently shake his head. I knew that the trip would always be our secret. Years went by and I became a passable architect, but hardly a successor to Gaudí. With his recommendation I obtained a position at the studio of Hector Guimard in Paris. It was there, almost two decades after that night in Manhattan, that I received the news of Gaudí's death. A tram had run him over on the Gran Vía as he returned to the Sagrada Familia after going to confession at his favourite church in the Gothic quarter of the old town. Passers-by had left him there bleeding for hours, thinking him a beggar. By the time his apprentices found him a day later, agonising in an asylum for the homeless, it was too late.

I took the first train to Barcelona, just in time to catch the funeral procession that would escort him on his last trip to the crypt of the Sagrada Familia, where I had met him and where he would be buried. That same day I sent a telegram to Hector Guimard in Paris announcing that I would not be returning. At dusk I retraced my steps to the church where I had first met Gaudí. Over the years the city had expanded around the site and the spires of my master's cathedral rose above it, reaching towards a sky splattered with stars. I closed my eyes, and for a second I could picture it finished, as Gaudí himself must have seen it in his mind.

I knew then I would dedicate my life to continuing my

master's work, realising that sooner or later I too would hand on the responsibility to others, and in time they would do the same. Because although God is patient, Gaudí, wherever he may be, is still waiting.

TWO-MINUTE APOCALYPSE

Written in English by Carlos Ruiz Zafón

The day the world ended I was standing at the corner of 5th and 57th checking my phone when a redhead with eyes of silver turned to me and said:

'Have you noticed how the smarter phones get, the dumber people become?'

She looked like a bride of Dracula fresh from a Goth shopping spree next door.

'Can I help you, miss?'

She said the world was coming to an end. Heavenly Legal had issued a malfunction recall and she was a fallen angel sent from below to ensure poor souls like mine found their way into the tenth circle of hell in an orderly fashion.

'I thought there were only nine circles down there,' I objected.

'We had to add one for all of those who've lived their lives as if they were going to live forever.'

I never took my medication seriously, but one look into those silver-dollar eyes and I knew she spoke the truth. Sensing my despair, she announced that since I had not worked in the financial sector I was to be granted three wishes before the big bang recanted and the universe imploded back into a cheerio.

'Pick wisely.'

I gave it some thought.

'I want to know the meaning of life, I want to know where I

can find the best chocolate ice cream ever and I want to fall in love,' I declared.

'The answer to your first two wishes is the same.'

As for the third, she gave me a kiss that tasted of all the truth in the world and made me want to be a decent man. We went for a goodbye walk in the Park and then we crossed the street and took the elevator to the top of the venerable Gothic-spired hotel to watch the world go in style.

'I love you,' I said.

'I know.'

We stood there, hand in hand, glancing at a furious tide of crimson clouds shrouding the skies, and I cried, happy at last.

ABOUT THE AUTHOR

Carlos Ruiz Zafón is the author of eight novels, including the internationally bestselling and critically acclaimed Cemetery of Forgotten Books series: *The Shadow of the Wind, The Angel's Game, The Prisoner of Heaven*, and *The Labyrinth of the Spirits*. His work, which also includes prizewinning young adult novels, has been translated into more than fifty languages and published around the world, garnering numerous awards and reaching millions of readers. *The City of Mist* is a collection of stories he prepared before his death in June 2020, meant to be published posthumously.

ALSO FROM
CARLOS RUIZ ZAFON

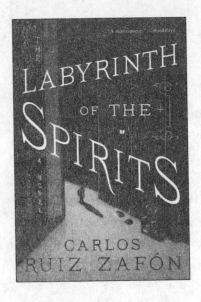

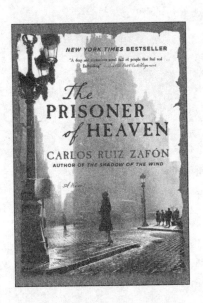